The Sleighbell Secret

Vanessa Lind

A holiday mystery that jingles all the way...

In an 1889 small town on the coast, intrepid newspaper reporter Jo Felch is swept up in holiday magic and mystery when she steps in to perform in the town's Christmas theatrical production. As props go missing and mishaps plague the show, Jo teams up with her former best friend to investigate the sabotage. Their list of suspects includes a spurned cast member, a disapproving reverend, and a new arrival to town with a troubled past.

When Jo and her partner discover the new woman is a former resident of the local orphanage that will benefit from the theatrical's proceeds, they wonder if old memories have sparked resentment strong enough to spur revenge. The secret of a missing sleighbell, buried grudges, and the true meaning of charity and forgiveness all play a part in this heartwarming historical mystery that evokes the spirit of the season.

CHAPTER ONE

Astoria, Oregon

1889

Stepping into the gray afternoon chill, Jo Felch locked the door of the *Astoria Evening Register* behind her. Well into her second year of running the newspaper, she still felt as if she was living a dream. Not even the well-known girl reporter Nellie Bly could boast of having full control of a paper. True, Jo had inherited the enterprise through unfortunate circumstances, and in this small but bustling Columbia River town, she had competition. All the same, she cherished the *Register*, and she took seriously her responsibilities as a publisher and a reporter.

As Christmas approached, the newspaper office was especially busy. Though tonight's edition was already out, the town's newsboys shouting its headlines from downtown street corners, Jo's pressman, Antero, was still at work inside the office, printing up Christmas advertisements and greeting cards for local businesses. The busy events of the town's social season meant the paper was crowded with writeups of community news, with coverage printed both before and after the events. Lately, Jo had been spending a good deal of time reminding folks that their submissions, no matter how socially significant, could not garner any more than the few lines allotted in the Local Happenings section. She was running a newspaper, after all, and her readers expected more than accounts of Christmas teas and parties, replete with descriptions of gowns and hats.

From her office, Jo made her way along the downtown boardwalk, her boots clacking on timbers cut from the Douglas firs that towered over the town's upper hillsides and beyond, a supply that seemed so endless as to furnish boardwalks like this for the entire planet. She stepped up her pace, invigorated by the air's wintery chill and the hum of activity in the commercial district. She dodged shoppers stopping to gawk at window displays, not just in the town's only department store but also in the dry goods store, the shoe store, and the milliner's shop. She passed several women juggling bags of toys and a man struggling with a Christmas tree, the crowd parting to make way for its sharp branches. In the street, sleighbells jingled on the horses of the expressmen, their wagons laden with packages to deliver. Boys blowing penny whistles and tin horns added to the pleasant cacophony.

Jo's own holiday shopping was nearly done, and a good thing, too, considering the tasks that loomed between now and Christmas day. She was having a handsome rocker built for her father, a cannery owner whose gout forced him to sit more than he'd like. She'd put a pretty night dress on hold for her friend Amity, who'd come from across the river to help her with the paper and, having fallen in love with a shipwrecked sailor, stayed on at Jo's house, sharing her bedroom in an arrangement that suited her and Jo both. For their maid, Effie, who'd cared for Jo since she was young, she'd found a pretty lace collar and thimble. For Pablo, the stowaway from Gus's ship who now helped Effie with her chores, she'd found a lovely pair of light blue silk suspenders. For Nan, the newspaper's typesetter, she'd purchased a pretty box lined with red silk, and for Antero, a burnt leather photograph case.

Most of all, Jo was pleased with the gift she'd found for Amity's brother, Noah, who managed the cannery for her father. Ever patient with her putting off his proposals of marriage, he deserved more than her money could buy. The fine silk umbrella she'd bought him, with silver filagree inlaid into its ivory handle, was but a token of her love.

The paper put to bed for the night and her gifts taken care of, she could now turn her attention to helping Noah with the props for the town's amateur Christmas theatrical, "The Magic at Mistletoe Manor." Amity had tried to get Jo, who'd starred in other theatricals when she was younger, to try out for a part in the production. But at the time of the casting, Jo hadn't been able to see her way clear at the newspaper in order to carve out the time necessary to learn a part. Assisting Noah took no preparation, and she shared the satisfaction of their joint behind-the-scenes effort.

Reaching the town's west end, Jo arrived at Ross's Opera House, one of Astoria's premier theatrical venues. Their little town was a regular stop on the touring company circuit, attracting some of the same shows that played in San Francisco.

Amateur productions like the Christmas theatrical kept the auditoriums full between the touring company stops.

Jo went around the front of the Opera House to the alley. As she tugged open the backstage door, a black cat lurking near a trash bin tried to worm its way inside. "Scat," she said, nudging the cat away with the toe of her boot. The cat meowed loudly in protest.

Nearby, a tortoise shell cat that was mostly all white gave a sympathetic yowl, striking Jo with a pang of guilt. "I know it's cold out here. I'd take you home, but Queenie would have a fit." Queenie was a small white dog that had won Pablo's heart when he was hiding aboard the ship that brought him from Mexico. "Next time, I'll bring something for you to eat, I promise."

Closing the door behind her, Jo found the backstage area a proverbial beehive of activity in preparation for today's dress rehearsal, the second of three. Playing the part of the benevolent Lord Mistletoe, Wesley Cunningham wore a powdered wig as he paced the floor, script in hand, reciting his lines. Nearby, Clara Shelton stood in front of a full-length mirror, adjusting the green collar of her forest sprite costume.

Looking over Clara's shoulder, a second sprite, played by Felicity Chambers, frowned at their reflections. "We look like elves, not sprites," Felicity said.

"Elves, sprites, what's the difference?" Dressed in a colorful outfit reminiscent of a court jester's garb, Will Storey, a surfman from the lifesaving station, came up behind them. The director had cast him as Jingle, a mischievous Christmas spirit unleashed by an enchanted book from Mistletoe Manor's neglected library. In an act of community spirit befitting the season, Will's commander at the lifesaving station had graciously granted him time for the production.

Will lifted each sprite's hand and kissed it, but his kiss lingered on Clara's fingers. Known for switching beaus almost as frequently as the ocean changed tides, Clara had been seeing Will since Thanksgiving, a span of weeks that had Jo teasing her about marriage.

Waving in greeting, Jo strode past them to where Noah's sister Amity sat at a dressing table, applying rouge to her cheeks. As Eliza Mistletoe, granddaughter of Lord Mistletoe, she had the lead role in the theatrical, joining forces with Jingle to defeat the Winter Witch, who had cast a spell over the manor, shrouding it in perpetual winter and stealing the joy from Christmas.

"Where's Noah?" Jo asked.

"Behind the wardrobe, last I saw him." Amity set down her brush and picked up a thinner one along with a pot of lipstick. "He's putting the finishing touches on the magic book."

"Still?" Jo said. "It looked fine to me last night."

"You know Noah. Either he does it to perfection or not at all."

There was no arguing that point. It was part of what made Noah such a good manager for Jo's father, despite his young age and the fact that he'd had to learn the job from scratch.

Crossing over to Noah's makeshift workshop behind the costume wardrobe, Jo passed Amity's beau, Gus. Dressed in a fancy suit, he looked every bit the part of the English gentleman which, according to rumor, he was. For his part, Gus was tight-lipped about his life before his ship went aground on Clatsop Sands. In his role as Nicholas, a mysterious visitor summoned by the ancient magic of the enchanted book, he was to wear a top hat, but at the moment, he was wrestling to keep it atop his head.

"Do you think I'm big-headed?" he asked Jo as she passed.

"Not especially."

"This hat seems to think so." He let go of the hat. It slipped to the floor, landing at her feet.

She stooped to retrieve it. "This looks like it was made to fit a child," she said, turning it around in her hands. "Probably left over from last year's Oliver Twist production. You can borrow one of Father's."

"Thank heavens," he said. "If my head was swelling, I fear Amity would want nothing more to do with me."

It would take a lot more than that for Amity to abandon Gus, Jo knew. She and Noah strongly suspected that Gus's gift to Amity this Christmas would be an engagement ring. According to Noah, Gus had been squirreling away nearly all his earnings at the mill, though he was wont to say what for.

Skirting the wardrobe, its doors splayed open and costumes turned every which-way inside, Jo found Noah bent over the worktable he'd set up. He was wrestling a swath of emerald green fabric over the cover of a large volume of Thackeray, a prop donated from Jo's father's extensive library.

"That book looked just fine yesterday." She pecked his cheek with a kiss.

Looking up, he smiled, but the look of concentration remained. "The blue didn't look right for Christmas. Put your finger on this corner, will you, so I can glue down the edges?"

She pressed her finger to the corner while he ran a line of glue along the edge of the fabric, then pressed it tight over the book. "What about the golden runes you'd attached?" she asked.

"I'm redoing them too. One was crooked."

"No one will notice from the audience."

"I'd notice." He patted the fabric, taut on the book's cover. "Paper come out all right?"

"To my standards." Noah was better off working with numbers and machines at the cannery than he would be running a newspaper. Jo placed a high value on getting things right, but with daily editions, there were bound to be errors now and then. Unlike her competitor, Randolph Jenkins at the *Astoria Morning Gazette,* she publicly acknowledged these faux pas in an errata section.

"See if you can find Jingle's staff, would you?" Noah said. "Will misplaced it somehow."

"Might be in the wardrobe. I'll have a look." She started that direction, but Noah stopped her.

"I almost forgot. Dorinda was here looking for you."

Jo suppressed a sigh. Living next door in a house nearly identical to Jo's, Dorinda Hamilton was the daughter of a rival cannery owner. Their fathers had once been fast friends, but they'd had a falling out while building their mansions. Nonetheless, their daughters had remained friends of a sort, at least while they were growing up. Jo had idolized Dorinda, who wore all the right clothes and knew all the right people. But when tragedy struck Jo's family and Jo's mother died, it was Amity who'd stuck by Jo, not Dorinda. As she recovered from her loss, Jo realized that Dorinda's self-confidence was shallower than it seemed, and her need for attention now grated on Jo's nerves.

"I don't know why she'd try to track me down here, unless it's about her Christmas charity fund. But we've covered it twice already in our Local Happenings column. I don't know what more she expects."

But even as she said this, Jo knew Dorinda always expected more.

Chapter Two

Coming home after the rehearsal, Jo was met at the door with the smell of cloved oranges. Pablo was on a ladder in the entry to the parlor, hanging a ribboned orange at Effie's direction. Beyond, Queenie lay curled on the parlor rug, oblivious to the fuss.

"Good evening, Miss Jo." From his perch, Pablo flashed a smile, his face lit by the warm glow of the foyer's gaslit sconce. Jo's father was planning to have the gas lights replaced soon with electric lighting. A convenience, to be sure, but Jo would miss the soft light and the gentle hiss of the gas fixtures.

"Good evening, Pablo."

"A little to the right," Effie said. Turning to Jo, she lowered her voice. "Thank heavens you're here. Dorinda Hamilton is waiting in the library. She's asked at least five times when you'd be home. She wants to talk with you. She says it's important."

"It must be." Jo shrugged out of her coat. "She never comes calling except on Wednesdays. But then her mother is likely still up in Seattle, tending to Dorinda's aunt. So I suppose the usual protocols can be adjusted."

"While the cat's away." Effie reached for Jo's wrap.

"I'll hang it," Jo said. "You tend to your decorations. They look lovely, by the way. You've gone all out this year."

Effie beamed. "Pablo cut lots of greenery. Brightens things up on these dreary winter days."

Lots of greenery didn't begin to describe it, Jo thought as she hung her coat in the hall closet. Sprigs of holly and boxwood intermingled with pine boughs festooned the bannisters of the grand staircase as well as the mantles of every fireplace. Crafted of holly, grapevines, dried fruit, and gilt berries, wreaths hung on every door. Passing the dining room, Jo admired the lace table runner on the big table, topped by a cornucopia overflowing with bright apples, nuts, and hard-necked squashes.

Steeling herself for Dorinda's entreaties, she proceeded to the library. From the top of the library's doorframe hung a sprig of mistletoe, Effie's not-so-subtle encouragement of the romantic relationships that Jo and Amity enjoyed with Noah and Gus. She would like nothing more than to turn her decorating talents on a pair of weddings next year.

A Douglas fir that reached to the ceiling, the grand Christmas tree in the library dwarfed all else in the room. Noah had tromped up the backside of Coxcomb Hill to cut it, then dragged it here. Strands of cranberries, dried fruit, and wrapped candies festooned the tree, its branches hung with tinsel and tatted snowflakes tied on with ribbons. Candle clips secured small white tapers the family would light on Christmas Eve.

Half-obscured by the tree, Dorinda was perched on the settee, sipping a cup of tea. As usual, she was dressed to the nines, in a deep mauve bustled skirt with lace-paneled accents.

"There you are." Seeing Jo, she set her teacup back in its saucer. "I've been looking for you everywhere."

Settling at the other end of the settee, Jo breathed in the sharp smell of evergreen. "Noah told me you stopped by the theatre."

"And your office. But that man said you'd already left."

"Antero. He runs our presses. You must have passed me on the street. I walked through downtown to Ross's."

"You walked in weather like this?" Dorinda gave an exaggerated shudder.

Jo shrugged. "A little chilly, but it's not wet or windy. For December, that passes for a stellar day."

Dorinda leaned forward. "You must know why I'm eager to speak with you."

"If it's about your Christmas charity effort, I'm afraid I've given it all the coverage I can at the paper."

Dorinda looked aghast at this news. "It's for the children, Jo. The orphans. And it's *Christmas.*"

"I know it's a worthy cause. But there are any number of worthy causes this season. We can't favor yours over anyone else's."

Dorinda's face tightened. "But how am I supposed to get donations without proper coverage in the paper?"

"You could go door to door."

"I can't go calling on strangers without Mother along. She's in Seattle, you know. Her sister is ill."

"Yes, I know. I'm sorry to hear it. But I can't imagine anyone would look askance at your going out on your own." Pausing, Jo noted Dorinda's horrified look. "On the proper day, of course. And with your calling cards."

Dorinda shook her head vehemently. “You don’t understand. There simply isn’t time.”

“What about your father? And Warren? They have connections among the more well-to-do set who are most likely to donate.”

“Father just got back from San Francisco, and he’s in a foul mood. I shan’t be asking him for anything for at least a week. And Warren...well, you know Warren,” Dorinda said.

Jo did know Warren Hatch. Quite well, as a matter of fact. A few years back, she and Warren, an up-and-coming local attorney, had been engaged to be married. Realizing how incompatible they were, Jo had broken it off. She wasn’t sure Warren had ever forgiven her. Not because he was so in love with her—she wasn’t sure he’d ever loved her at all, only loved the idea of marrying into one of Astoria’s wealthiest families. Now, with Dorinda, he was close to achieving that goal. Dorinda could be something of a force of nature, not so different from the gales that blew in off the ocean this time of year, so Warren had little choice but to give her free rein in a way he never seemed to manage when he was with Jo. He was a bright man with a promising future, but observing his passivity around Dorinda, Jo worried that one day, without warning, he’d erupt, like a volcano.

But none of that was Jo’s concern right now. She was tired and hungry and her feet ached. She wanted to rid herself of Dorinda so she could relax over supper with her father and Amity, who would be home after she finished a Christmas errand downtown.

“I don’t know what else to tell you, Dorinda. Even if we had the space to give your efforts more coverage in the paper, there's no guarantee people would donate. Lots of charities are clamoring for attention this time of year."

"That's not how Joseph Pulitzer sees it," Dorinda said indignantly. "He set up a Christmas Tree fund in St. Louis and promotes it in his newspaper, raising funds to provide food and toys to tens of thousands of needy children. I know because I read an item about it in your *Register.*"

Jo remembered the item, a snippet from the wire service that they ran to fill an empty space between advertisements. "I'm afraid I'm no Joseph Pulitzer."

"But you could be, Jo, if you'd just devote yourself to this cause. The Hartfield Children's Home has a storied history. It was founded nearly forty years ago to care for children who were orphaned when their families crossed the Oregon Trail. Do you have any idea the hardships those poor babes faced? Floods. Famine. Disease. Attacks by Indians. Many saw their parents die right before their eyes."

"I've read some accounts," Jo said. "I'm sure it was horrific. But those children are grown now. They're out on their own."

"Which could only have happened because the folks at the Children's Home stepped in and helped. And they could only help because of the generosity of those who filled their coffers. Up the river in Weston, they're practically our neighbors. And between you and me, the Home's prospects aren't looking good. When Portland people donate to charity, they stick to causes closer to home. If we don't step up, the Home could close."

One thing about Dorinda—she could be persuasive. "I'll speak to Father about it," Jo said. "I'm sure he'll make a donation."

"He already has." Morosely, Dorinda shook her head. "We need more. Much more. And Christmas is only days away."

Jo sat silently for a moment. Staring at the Christmas tree, with its candles and tinsel, she thought of how fortunate she'd been, growing up in this home, surrounded by love and wanting for nothing. There was no question that the Hartfield Children's Home was a worthy cause. Jo had lost her own mother when she was only seventeen, a huge blow from which she'd struggled to recover. She couldn't imagine having to deal with such a loss at a younger age, not to mention the death of not just one parent, but two. On top of that, the Oregon Trail orphans had landed in a place that was utterly foreign to them, with hundreds of miles of mountains and deserts separating them from the places where they'd been born.

She glanced over at Dorinda. Biting her lip, she seemed on the verge of tears. She certainly had her faults. So did Jo. At least during this holiday season, Dorinda was striving to do some good in the world. Cynically, Jo might tell herself that Dorinda was doing this for the same reason she did most things, to garner attention. But she had to admit that there was an unusually selfless aspect to this appeal. And it was Christmas, after all. There had to be some way to help Dorinda without compromising what Jo did at her newspaper.

"I've got an idea," she said. "How about you ask Oliver Hastings to donate a portion of the ticket sales from the theatrical to your cause? It's an amateur production. No one's getting paid, and from what I understand, he has made similar donations from the proceeds of past theatricals. If he agrees, we can add the bit about raising funds to the advertisements we run in the paper for the theatrical. You'll get extra visibility, and people will be more motivated to purchase tickets if they know the money is going to a good cause."

Dorinda's face lit up. She pressed her hands together in front of her chest. "That's brilliant, Jo. You'll help, won't you? Introduce me to Mr. Hastings, put in a good word, and he'll simply have to go along with it."

"I'll do what I can." Jo was beginning to feel as Warren must, that it was easier to go along with Dorinda's wishes than to argue. "Come by the theatre tomorrow, and I'll introduce you before the rehearsal gets underway."

Chapter Three

When Jo arrived at the Opera House for the next dress rehearsal, Dorinda was waiting at the door. The front door, of course, because the Hamiltons weren't accustomed to frequenting alleyways. Parked behind her was her father's carriage, the coachman blowing warm air into his cupped hands, warding off the cold.

Knowing that using the backstage door would be a bridge too far for Dorinda, Jo waved at her, then went around through the back. Weaving past actors in various states of preparation, she proceeded onto the stage. From this vantage point, the elegance of the Opera House was impressive to behold. Inlaid into the stucco walls and set off with gilded frames were scenes from classical mythology. Echo and Narcissus. Cupid and Psyche. Midas and his gold. The Argonauts. The theme continued over the high ceiling, where inset panels depicted colorful renderings of Persephone, Hercules, and Zeus.

She descended the stairs to the orchestra section, then proceeded up the aisle of the auditorium. Looking over the empty seats, Jo was amazed as always that a town this size could draw a crowd of two thousand to performances. Not that they expected that many people for the Christmas theatrical. Then again, you never knew, especially since it would only run for four nights.

Like the auditorium, the lobby was elegant, with velvet-flecked wallpaper and big potted plants that gave the illusion of summer no matter the season. Jo pushed open one of the big entry doors, letting in a blast of cold air.

"I thought you'd never get here," Dorinda said crossly as she stepped inside. "It's freezing out here."

"Technically speaking, there's no ice," Jo said. "But after tonight, there could be." Mostly, Astoria's winters were free of ice and snow, but on occasion, when warm and cold fronts collided near the Columbia River's wide mouth, the townspeople got a taste of real winter. One year, a cold spell had lasted so long that the river, four miles wide between here and Washington Territory on the far side, had nearly frozen over.

"I certainly hope it doesn't freeze." Dorinda stamped her feet lightly on the rug, as if to warm them. "Think what that would do to attendance." Already, Jo could see, she was linking the success of the theatrical to the success of her charity effort, at least in her mind.

"We'd best hurry if we're to speak with Mr. Hastings before the rehearsal begins." Jo started for the auditorium. Trailing behind, Dorinda craned her neck, taking in her surroundings. "I've never been in here when it's empty. It seems so...grand. And also lonely." She spoke as if she was familiar with loneliness. But that was ridiculous. Dorinda Hamilton was the most social person Jo knew.

Their boots clacking rhythmically, they crossed the wooden stage. Jo held back the thick velvet curtain, and they ducked behind it. Oliver Hastings was still standing where Jo had seen him on her way through, speaking in an animated fashion to Jingle and the two forest sprites. In his early forties, Hastings had for years been the dedicated but somewhat scatterbrained director of many of the town's amateur productions. With a perpetually disheveled appearance, his clothes often seemed to have leaped from his closet onto his lanky frame of their own accord. But when it came to putting on a show, his creativity was unmatched. Jo had often marveled how, with some sort of alchemy of costumes, set, and aptly delivered lines teased from the lips of the actors, he could transform ordinary scenes into fabled spectacles.

"You are the gatekeepers of this production's enchantment," he was saying to Jingle and the sprites as Jo and Dorinda approached. "Look mischievous. Tilt your heads, like this, so the light glints off your eyes." He demonstrated, cocking his head to one side and then the other. Behind his glasses, perched precariously on the end of his nose, his blue eyes sparkled.

Clara, Felicity, and Will mimicked his movement. Will formed his mouth into an O, an exaggerated expression of amazement at something only he could see.

"Yes, yes!" Hastings clapped his hands. "That's it. Now for your movements. You must prance along with a light step, almost as if you're on tiptoe, but with a bounce to it, as if you can't wait to see what's around the next corner. Like this." Shifting his weight to his toes, the director demonstrated, circling them as a spirited horse might. "Now you try."

The actors exchanged glances. Will set off in such a spirited prance that Clara burst out laughing.

"Good, good," Hastings said. "Now the ladies."

Recovering herself, Clara followed Will's example. Felicity brought up the rear, though with a decidedly grumpy cadence to her prance. She'd auditioned for the theatrical's lead role, and from what Jo had observed, she still resented the fact that Hastings had chosen Amity instead.

Hastings broke into applause. "That's the spirit!" he exclaimed, focusing on Will and Clara instead of Felicity. "Now go finish with your makeup." He made a shooing motion with his hands. "Rehearsal begins in ten minutes."

With the fondness of a father seeing three young children off to school, he stood watching as Jingle and his sprites headed for the dressing tables.

"Mr. Hastings." Jo tapped his shoulder. "If you have a moment, there's someone here who'd like a word with you."

Startled out of his reverie, Hastings turned. "Ah, the Hamilton girl," he said. "All the parts are spoken for, I'm afraid. But we'll have another production coming up in the spring."

Poised as ever, Dorinda stepped forward. "I haven't come about a part, Mr. Hastings. I'm raising funds for the Hartfield Children's Home this Christmas season. You're familiar with the orphanage and its mission, I presume?"

Reaching through his unruly brown hair, he scratched his head. "The orphanage. Yes, yes. In Knappton, is it?"

"Weston," Dorinda said. "The Home opened in 1862 to assist children who were orphaned when their families crossed the Oregon Trail."

He shook his head. "So many hardships. I worked with an actor once who'd made that journey as a child. Or perhaps it was his father. I don't recall."

"It could have been either," Jo said, hoping to move the conversation along. "The route was used for decades until the railroads came through."

"As you can imagine, in a facility that has been around for that many years, maintenance is needed," Dorinda said. "And though the trail is no longer in use, there are sadly many orphans still with us today. Without families to care for them, they need a place to stay until they're of an age to fend for themselves. That's why I've taken on their cause this Christmas. But with so many distractions this time of year, the donations aren't coming in as I'd like. I was telling Jo about it, and she said you could help."

Jo shot Dorinda a look. "I said you'd be willing to hear Dorinda's appeal, Mr. Hastings. And I suggested that perhaps a portion of each night's ticket sales could go toward the charity drive. If you're agreeable, I could adjust the notices in the paper to reflect that. It might encourage folks to turn out for the production."

"Splendid idea." Hastings pushed his glasses up the bridge of his nose. "Twenty percent to the Children's Home?"

"Twenty-five percent," Dorinda said.

He drew back, looking surprised. "Well...it is for the children, I suppose. Twenty-five percent."

"Thank you, Mr. Hastings." Dorinda grabbed his hand and pumped it. "On behalf of the children and staff of the Hartfield Children's Home."

"I'll leave you two to work out the details," he said with a dismissive wave of his hand. "I've got enough to see to with this show."

"I'll come each night and explain from the stage how the donations will be used," Dorinda said.

Of course she would. Because that would put her at the center of things.

"I'm not sure that will be necessary," Jo said. "What do you think, Mr. Hastings?"

Glancing at his pocket watch, he seemed not to hear.

"So it's all decided," Dorinda said.

Such was the course of things when Dorinda was involved. At least in this case, her being in the spotlight would benefit someone else.

"I need to get going," Jo told her. "Noah needs my help with the props. You can sit out there if you like." She gestured toward the auditorium. "Get a preview of the show."

"Not now," Dorinda said. "My carriage is waiting, and I'll need to get home and pick out a gown to wear each night. Theatrical people pay such attention to appearances."

But as she turned to leave, Hastings gestured for her to come close. "Cast meeting, everyone! Miss Hamilton! Do say a word to the actors about your splendid effort."

Regally, Dorinda approached the assembled actors and stagehands. Though nearly all were friends and acquaintances, she spoke to them as if she had arrived from another town to enlighten them. In a speech that went on too long, she talked about the Children's Home and its needs. She explained the fundraising arrangement and thanked them in advance for their participation.

As she launched into an accounting of the Home's finances, feet began shuffling, the actors growing antsy to make their final preparations before the rehearsal began in earnest. Hastings cleared his throat. "Thank you, Miss Hamilton," he said, cutting her off.

If Dorinda was offended, she didn't show it. "Break a leg," she said. With a little wave, she left them to play their parts.

Chapter Four

Once Dorinda was gone, the stagehands went to work, putting the finishing touches on the set for the opening scene. The scene's actors took their places. Setting off to help Noah ready the props for the next scene, Jo nearly ran into her friend Fannie, clad in the Winter Witch's white cloak.

"Sorry. I didn't..." Fannie coughed, sniffled, then coughed again. Even through the white grease paint, Jo could see that her face was flushed.

"Are you all right?" Jo said.

"Not really." Fannie sneezed. "My head is pounding, and I feel like I've got a fever. I think it's the grippe. My little brother came down with it a couple of days ago."

"You should go home," Jo said. "Rest up for opening night. You hardly have any lines. I'm sure someone could stand in for you till then."

"I already asked Fel—" She broke into a coughing fit. "Felicity," she said, recovering. "She doesn't want to play a witch. And she pointed out that there's a scene with the witch and the sprites, so it wouldn't work anyhow."

"What about Tilly?" The wife of Gus's boss, the new manager at the mill, Tilly O'Malley had only recently joined the cast, not as an actor but as a vocalist. "She only has the two songs."

"And the Winter Witch is onstage for one of them." With this, another coughing fit ensued.

Hastings rushed toward them. "Is something wrong?"

"Fannie thinks she's coming down with the grippe," Jo said as Fannie tried to squelch her cough.

"Where's the understudy?" Hastings looked from left to right as if one was lurking nearby.

"There aren't any understudies," Jo said.

"Oh," he said. "Right. Well, Fannie, my advice is to get to bed and rest. Hot honey and lemon, that's the thing for that cough."

"But the..." Her voice was shaky. "The Winter Witch. Who'll play her?"

"I suppose I could do it," Jo said. "Noah doesn't need much help with the props. And there are only a few lines."

"You just have to glower," Hastings said. "Like this." He made a face, pursing his lips and furrowing his brow.

Jo imitated the look.

"Splendid. And swing your arms around thusly." Still making the face, he crouched slightly, sweeping his arms through the air as he emitted an evil laugh.

Jo followed suit, undulating her arms as if through them she wielded a powerful spell over Mistletoe Manor, which was precisely the point.

Ten minutes later, she found herself onstage, garbed in the white cloak of the Winter Witch, her face covered with white grease paint.

"Final rehearsal," Hastings said, belting out instructions. "Jingle and sprites, I want you stepping lively. Lord Mistletoe, remember to lean on your cane." He frowned. "Where is it, by the way?"

"Coming," Noah called from backstage.

"Good, good," Hastings said. "Now Eliza, an expression of utter amazement, please, when you open the enchanted book."

Amity nodded. "Amazement."

"And Nicholas, you must be downcast when Jingle first drags you onto the scene. No lighting up when you see Eliza."

"I'll do my best, sir." Gus tipped his top hat, borrowed from Jo's father, at the director.

Hastings frowned, his brow furrowed. "Where's my church mouse?"

"Mouse in the Corner, sir." Dressed in a furry gray suit and with whiskers drawn on her face, Tilly O'Malley stepped from the wings. "Sorry I'm late."

"Just so you don't come down with the grippe," Hastings said. "Can anyone else here carry a tune?"

Will Storey stepped forward. "I can sing with enthusiasm."

His friends laughed, enthusiasm being the kindest way to describe Will's propensity for breaking into song.

Coming from the props area, Noah handed Wesley his cane. "Not sure you'd fit into that mouse costume, Will."

"Then our mouse had best stay healthy." Hastings clapped his hands twice, signaling the official start of rehearsal. "Act One, Scene One. Places, everyone."

The drama began. With the Witch not coming onstage until Act Two, Jo waited in the wings beside Noah, who was lining up props for the next scene. "Your book looks fabulous," she said as Amity's character, Eliza, pulled it from the dusty shelf in the Mistletoe Manor library, where the first scene was set. "With the gold foil runes, it looks so mysterious."

"Thanks. And you make a stellar Winter Witch. I fear I've already fallen under your spell." A candlestick in one hand, Noah planted a kiss on her cheek. He came away with white paint from her face on his lips, an effect that caused her to have to stifle a giggle.

Smudging the grease paint back over the spot where he'd kissed her, Jo turned her attention to the book-finding scene unfolding onstage.

"What a curious book." With the look of utter amazement Hastings had requested, Amity traced her fingers over the gold foil runes. "I wonder where it came from."

With a slow, deliberate movement meant to heighten anticipation, she opened the book's cover and turned a page, sending up a cloud of dust that Jo knew was actually face powder.

Cued by the dust cloud, Will leaped from the wings in his Jingle suit. In an exaggerated motion, he rubbed his eyes with his fisted hands. "What a long sleep I've had. I thought no one was ever going to—"

"Hold it right there," a voice called out. Mounting the stairs at the foot of the stage, Reverend Henry Worthington strode toward Amity and Will, his footsteps reverberating on the wooden platform. Charged with the spiritual guidance of one of Astoria's largest congregations, he was a stern-looking man with a prominent jawline and piercing gray eyes. Folding his arms at his chest, he turned his gaze on the actors. "Christmas is a time for reflection and reverence, not frivolity and enchantment."

Amity and Will exchanged nervous glances.

"This sort of flippant entertainment during the holy season will lead our community astray," he continued. "You must abandon this production immediately."

The book open in her arms, Amity drew herself up, meeting the reverend's gaze. "If you'll stay and watch the rehearsal, Reverend, you'll see that this production is not without moral merit. Like the Bible, this book unlocks—"

"I shall not waste my time on such drivel," he interrupted. "And to compare your *enchanted* book to our holy one is akin to blasphemy."

"But both tell of love and redemption," Amity continued, undaunted.

"And a little frivolity now and then can be good for the soul." In his jester's outfit, Will made a little leap, twirling in the air and landing gracefully on his feet.

The reverend's frown deepened. "I'll be the judge of what's good for the soul."

"Reverend Worthington, we do so appreciate your interest in our little production." From his seat in the auditorium, Oliver Hastings approached the stage. Standing in the darkened orchestra area, he looked small, the reverend towering over him from the platform. "In honor of the season, perhaps you'd consider playing a small part yourself."

"A part!" The reverend's voice thundered. "The only part I shall play is as the voice of God in our church's own pageant on Christmas Eve. Though I expect this year's attendance will be down if people opt to attend your...your spectacle instead."

"Oh, I didn't mean a part in the play itself." Hastings steepled his hands. "I thought you might say an invocation before each night's performance."

Worthington straightened. "I'm a busy man, Mr. Hastings."

"It's only four nights," Amity said. "And of course you wouldn't be expected to stay for the show."

"An invocation would go a long way toward invoking the proper spirit." This time, Will refrained from any exuberant display. "Reflective. Reverent."

Worthington's gaze softened a bit. "I suppose an invocation would fall within the realm of my duties. In service to the community."

"Splendid," Hastings said. "Come at quarter of seven tomorrow. You'll be first onstage."

"Very well." Worthington looked from one wing to the other, where the other actors were assembled. "And I trust that I shall see some if not all of you in the audience for our pageant this year." With that, he turned and left, disappearing into the darkness of the auditorium.

"I don't see what he's worried about," Jo whispered to Noah. "His church is always packed to overflowing for the Christmas Eve pageant. I've been attending since I was five years old."

"Me too," Noah said. "Till we moved across the river."

"I don't recall him making a fuss about last year's theatrical," Jo said.

"You heard how he said *enchanted* book. Maybe that's the rub."

"I suppose it could be. But how does he know enough about the show to know the book is enchanted?"

Noah shrugged. "Small town. Word gets around."

"I just hope he hasn't run off half our audience, ranting about it to his parishioners."

"Wait till he finds out about the Winter Witch." Grinning, he lifted a strand of her powdered hair.

The interruption dealt with, Hastings got the rehearsal going again. All went smoothly from there. Hobbling across the stage with his cane, Wesley played a superb Lord Mistletoe. For the first time, Felicity managed to show a degree of frivolity worthy of a sprite. Jo hoped she'd finally let go of her resentment of Amity playing the part of Eliza. In the middle of Act Two, Tilly's Mouse in the Corner sang "In the Bleak Midwinter" with such clarity and depth that Jo found herself feeling genuinely mournful over the Manor's fate.

As promised, playing the part of the Winter Witch wasn't hard. In fact, it was rather fun, moving her arms about with wild abandon while cackling and making threatening faces. The lines were easy too. "This Manor is mine, all mine." Then, later in the act, "My spell shall never be broken." And in Act Three, when love prevailed over arrogance, "Ruined! I'm ruined!"

When the cast and stage crew all gathered around the sleigh at the end of Act Three, Tilly leading them in a final song, Jo felt a surge of joy. The tinsel, the tin horns, the tree, and the gifts—nothing said Christmas like sharing an accomplishment with her friends.

"Never a cast like this one," Hastings raved when the singing ended. "The magic of Christmas! The heartfelt triumph of love!" At this last exclamation, Amity and Gus exchanged smiles. Their onstage kiss, breaking the Witch's spell, didn't need to be staged. It was genuine.

Hastings gave a few final reminders of how things would proceed during the four nights of performances. After that, everyone scattered, the actors to peel out of their costumes and rub the makeup off their faces, the stagehands to break down the last set and arrange the opening one for tomorrow. All of them working together toward a single goal, bringing joy to the people of their town.

Jo made her way to the dressing table. Greased and dusted with powder, her face felt heavy, and every time her hand inadvertently went to her hair, it came away white. As she neared the moment of her relief, she passed Noah, who was digging through a pile of props.

“Looking for something?” she asked.

“The green book,” he said. “I could’ve sworn I put it right here after the library scene.”

“Maybe someone stuck it in the wardrobe.” Jo opened the doors and reached inside, feeling around the costumes with her hand while trying not to spread powder over them. No book.

“In a drawer, maybe?” Noah said.

“Worth a look.” They headed in different directions, opening and closing the drawers of every piece of furniture on the set. Save for a pencil and a random feather, Jo found nothing.

Removing her rouge at a dressing table, Amity caught Jo’s eye in the mirror. “It’s great that you’re embracing your role as the Witch. But I advise your getting that makeup off your face. After a while, it cakes on, and it doesn’t exactly do wonders for your complexion.”

“I’m trying to help Noah find the green book,” Jo said. “Have you seen it?”

“Not since Act One,” Amity said. “Jingle snatches it away, remember? He tosses it stage right. Didn’t anyone pick it up?”

“Noah thought he did. But it’s not where he recalls putting it.”

Amity frowned. "My brother has his flaws, but forgetfulness isn't one of them."

"Let's not get into a list of the others," Noah said, coming up behind Jo.

She whirled around. "No book?"

"No sign of it. Looks as if you had the same luck."

"It has to be here somewhere," Amity said. "It can't just have walked off."

"That's not all," Noah said. "I was checking around the sleigh from Act Three. I thought maybe the book somehow got tucked under the lap robe. There's a sleighbell missing."

"Just one sleighbell?" Jo asked. "Not the whole strip?" Absent a horse, stagehands pushed the sleigh onstage during the set change between Act Two and Act Three. From the opposite end of the stage, they pulled a rope as the next scene opened, dragging the sleigh over a set of removable tracks Noah had designed. To add to the impression of motion, he'd attached a strip of bells to either side of the sleigh. These made a pleasant jingling sound as the sleigh eased over the tracks.

"Nope." Noah ran his hand through his hair, clearly perplexed. "The rest of the sleighbells are in place. Only one looks like it's been cut off."

"We can get by without one sleighbell," Amity said. "But we have to find that book. The whole show revolves around it."

"That *enchanted* book," Jo said. "You heard the reverend's disdain when he said it. He didn't like your comparing it to the Bible."

"You think he took it?" Noah said.

"It's possible. Between Act One and Act Two, you and the rest of the crew are busy backstage with the scene change. He could have come in through the backstage door and grabbed it."

"Reverend Worthington doesn't seem the type to go around stealing books," Amity said.

"Maybe in his mind, he just borrowed it," Jo said. "To make a point."

"At my expense," Noah said glumly. "I could find another book and cover it except that I used the last of that green fabric. There's no more gold foil for cutting out runes either. It will just have to be plain."

Seeing how discouraged he looked, Jo squeezed his hand. "Don't go to too much trouble. It could still turn up."

But even as she said this, she had her doubts. Reverend Worthington had agreed to an invocation. But that didn't mean he was above sabotaging their production so his own pageant would shine.

Chapter Five

Gazing up at the soaring bell tower of Reverend Henry Worthington's church, Jo hoped coming here wasn't a mistake. Her father was on good terms with Worthington, and with Jo's last-minute recruitment to play the Winter Witch, the reverend likely had no idea she was involved in the production. The smart thing was to leave him thinking that.

Besides, did she really think a religious leader would stoop to something so petty as stealing an important prop to sabotage a production? She'd like to think not. Yet she'd known people to do all sorts of things on impulse, herself included. By paying the reverend a visit, she might be doing him a favor, giving him an opportunity to come clean.

If he'd taken the book and it wasn't impulsive, there was even more reason for her to intervene. Hastings had been clever, deflecting the reverend's criticism by involving him in the production. But this also had the potential to backfire. Given full control of the stage at the program's opening, Reverend Worthington could say whatever he chose about the production. If he made a convincing enough case for it being shut down, The Magic at Mistletoe Manor could end up being a one-night show.

Either way, the best course was to get a feel for what the reverend was thinking. Tugging on the handle of the heavy oaken door, Jo let herself into the sanctuary. Between the ceiling that seemed to reach for the heavens and the colorful play of light through the massive stained glass windows, she felt her breath catch in her throat, the sanctuary invoking awe.

Stepping lightly, she approached the reverend's office at the south end of the foyer. With equal lightness, she rapped on the door.

Through the heavy wood came the reverend's muffled voice, more command than invitation. "Enter."

She let herself in. As in the rest of the church, the air in the office felt almost as cool as the outside air. A musty odor tickled her nostrils, the smell of a building which, grand though it was, was void of life most of the week, save for this solitary man seated at his broad desk, a Bible open before him and a pen in his hand. His brow was furrowed, but it seemed to Jo in a more studious way than last night, when anger had etched his face.

"Miss Felch." Offering a smile, Worthington set down his pen. "Please, have a seat. To what do I owe the pleasure?"

Smoothing her skirt beneath her, she settled into one of two straight-backed chairs facing his desk. As she did so, she scanned the books on the tall shelf behind him but saw no sign of the green volume Noah had so carefully recovered. Then again, if the reverend had taken it, he'd not be likely to put it on display.

"I thought you might have some information to share about the church's annual Christmas Eve pageant," she said.

"We'd be happy to run a notice about it in the paper as we did last year."

His smile faded. "Mrs. Worthington was to have dropped that information at the *Register*'s office. Perhaps she forgot. She has become rather forgetful of late."

Effie had mentioned as much. On a recent Sunday, the reverend's wife had forgotten her name, even though Effie had been attending church there for years.

"I thought it might have gotten overlooked. If you'd like to jot down a few lines about this year's event, I'll see what I can put together."

"I can do better than that." Shuffling through a stack on his desk, he pulled out a sheet of paper and handed it to her. "That's the program, with the names of all who are participating."

"Perfect." She folded the paper and slipped it into her reticule. "This will run nicely alongside our notice about the community production of The Magic at Mistletoe Manor.

He frowned. "There's little connection between our pageant and that frivolous show."

"Oh, but this year that frivolous show is raising money for a cause that I expect you and your parishioners would be happy to support. You're familiar with the Hartfield Children's Home?"

"More than familiar. The founder, Cordelia Hartfield, worships here. Or she used to. These days, she doesn't get out much."

This bit of information threw Jo off her script. "I didn't realize the Home's founder lived in Astoria."

"You're far from the only one. As I said, she doesn't get out much. All those years tending to the needs of orphans took quite a toll on her, I expect. Still, she's a delightful person."

An idea came to Jo, one that would keep Reverend Worthington firmly on the side of their production, no matter his objections. "Do you think Miss Hartfield would consider attending the show's final performance? She could receive the donated funds on behalf of the Children's Home, assuming she still has some association there."

"Some association." He chuckled. "Her home is filled with memorabilia from her years at the Home. I'm not sure that woman has ever thrown away anything of sentimental value."

"Understandable, since she devoted her life to the children."

"I suppose. To your question, I expect she'd be delighted to attend, assuming her health allows. Would you like me to broach the question with her?"

"Yes, please. And if she'd consider an interview for the newspaper, I'd be most grateful." A report on a woman who'd devoted her life to helping orphans would be perfect for the days leading up to Christmas.

"Very well. I'll send a note by your office with her response. Assuming she agrees to attend the performance, she'll need an escort. As I indicated, she's rather frail these days."

"I don't know that I can personally escort her." Jo wasn't about to mention the reason was that she would be made up and costumed as the Winter Witch. "But I expect Dorinda Hamilton would be happy to take on that role. She's the one organizing the charity drive."

"Splendid," he said. "The Hamiltons are nothing if not reliable. Offering in the collection plate every Sunday, whether they're in attendance or not."

That was Baxter Hamilton, spreading his generosity around town so that all would acknowledge what an upstanding citizen he was. Jo's father donated to plenty of causes himself, including Reverend Worthington's church, but he preferred to do so anonymously.

Satisfied with the success of her mission, even if she hadn't put her hands on the book, Jo left for the newspaper office. *Her* newspaper office. She wasn't the only woman to own a newspaper. In Portland, Melvina Lockwood ran a paper with a regionwide circulation. Nor could Jo take credit for having founded her paper, the way Melvina had started up hers. But a day rarely went by that Jo didn't feel the pleasure of accomplishment from an enterprise that elevated her sense of purpose. Dorinda's annual charity drive must do the same for her, even if it was only for a few weeks out of the year.

Filled with activity, the day flew by. With Amity's help, Jo redid the front-page layout to accommodate a larger than usual police sale notice. Moving some of the wire stories to page two and foregoing others, they were able to squeeze in all the paid advertisements, which were substantial at this time of year, while also adding a few lines about the church's Christmas pageant to the Local Happenings section.

With apologies to Nan, the paper's typesetter, Jo altered the notice for The Magic at Mistletoe Manor to include an additional line about the charity connection with the Hartfield Children's Home. Every alteration in an existing block of the paper meant Nan had to redo the tedious typesetting of the text. With any luck, Jo hoped to ease her job in the coming year by purchasing a linotype machine like the one her competitor, Randolph Jenkins, had acquired for his operation.

Once the presses were rolling, Jo and Amity ducked out for the day. Amity went straight to the theatre to meet up with Gus before the rest of the cast rolled in. "Have to keep the love scene fresh and vibrant," Amity explained with a wink. Jo went by her house to change shoes, the white slippers Fannie had worn being a size too small. On her way out, she picked up the supper basket Effie had readied, filled with enough sandwiches and cookies to feed half the cast plus a tin of milk for the alley cats.

The basket heavy on her arm, Jo proceeded to the theatre. Like Dorinda, she might have gone by carriage had she arranged in advance with her father's coachman. But these days, her father relied heavily on the carriage, his gout making it difficult for him to walk more than a few yards at a stretch. And Jo didn't mind the fresh air. If it was raining cats and dogs, as it often did this time of year, she'd take the streetcar, where she picked up snippets of local gossip that sometimes led to news stories.

This afternoon, the sun dropping toward where the gray sky met the gray river, the air was dry, or mostly so. But as Jo neared the theatre, rain began to fall in earnest. She hurried along, not minding a bit of damp but wanting to avoid getting soaked.

As she reached the backstage door, she spotted the cats huddled beneath the eaves. "Stay close," she said. "I'll be out in a minute with a treat."

She edged through the doorway, not wanting her feline friends to get any ideas about coming inside. It was a little late to be scripting two cats into the theatrical. Taking Jo's basket,

Amity unpacked the egg salad sandwiches, cut into triangles, and set the small plates on a cloth tossed over a wooden crate. Using the opener Effie had packed, Jo punched a hole in the milk tin. Grabbing a bowl from the prop cabinet, she went back outside. The rain shower was waning, and she was able to pour the milk into the bowl without getting soaked to the skin.

"Drink up," she said. Creeping from beneath the eaves, the cats circled the bowl, sniffing warily. As Jo started back into the theatre, they began lapping furiously at the milk.

With Noah, Gus, and Amity, Jo enjoyed the indoor picnic Effie had packed. But they all admitted to being too jittery to eat as much as they otherwise might—even Gus, who had a hearty appetite. As the rest of the cast trickled in, they shared what was left of the meal. When they'd finished, there was little to pack back in the basket. A good thing, as Effie took offense when the food she'd prepared came back uneaten.

Then the actors were off to don their costumes and makeup. While Jo got into her costume, Noah made one more sweep of the props area, searching for the book.

"Any luck?" she asked, emerging from the dressing room.

He shook his head. "It's like it vanished into thin air. The book and the sleighbell both. Must be the magic of Mistletoe Manor."

Jo was glad he wasn't dwelling on the mishap, which in the larger scheme of things wasn't all that disruptive. "I went to see Reverend Worthington this morning," she said.

"And made a thorough search of his office, I presume?"

She laughed. "I'm not that bold. But I got to thinking that he might be tempted to take advantage of Mr. Hastings' invitation. In his invocation, he's free to say whatever he likes, even if it reflects poorly on the show."

"And if word got around, no one would come to the rest of the performances."

"Exactly. No one wants to get on the wrong side of a man of the cloth. But I think I found a way to appease him. I told him about how a portion of the ticket sales will go to support the Hartfield Children's Home. As it turns out, the Home's founder is part of his congregation. He's going to see if she'd like to attend the final performance so we can recognize her efforts."

"Amazing. You've got him all on our side now." Taking her into his arms, Noah swung her around, her white robe ballooning out around her.

"That still doesn't fix the problem with the book," she said as he set her back on her feet.

"I brought a substitute tome from the cannery office." He lifted a thick brown book from a side table that was part of the Act One library scene.

"*Pacific Coast Fisheries,*" Jo read from the cover. "That adds a fresh twist to the Mistletoe Magic."

Noah shrugged. "From the audience, no one will be able to read the title."

It must be the spirit of the season, she thought as she went to her dressing table, Noah easing up on his expectations of himself.

Jo felt bad for Fannie, who according to her older brother's report was feeling only marginally better and was still confined to bed. At the same time, she savored the thrill of being part of the opening night's excitement. From the wings, she watched as the auditorium filled up. Not every seat was taken, but a good number were, filled by men, women, and children decked out in their holiday best. Aside from the comfort of home and hearth, nowhere but a theatre could contain so much happy anticipation, she thought.

As the performance time drew near, notes floated up from the orchestra, the oboes and flutes and violins warming up. The conductor raised his baton, and the discordant notes ceased, the musicians striking up a portion of what had to be Beethoven's best-known symphony, commonly called "Ode to Joy."

Across the stage, in the opposite wing, Oliver Hastings paced the floor, his hands behind his back. Having donned a suit and, from the looks of it, run a comb through his hair, he looked almost respectable. As the cast arranged themselves for the opening scene, Reverend Worthington joined the director backstage. Breaking his stride, Hastings patted the reverend on the back, the two of them exchanging what looked to be pleasantries. Moments later, Dorinda joined them. In her sweeping crimson gown, she looked like the belle of the ball.

Jo glanced at the backstage clock. "Three minutes," she said to Amity, who'd come alongside her. "You look glorious, by the way." For all Dorinda's elegance, there was a fresh sincerity about Amity that gave her an authentic sort of glow, even without the makeup.

"Not too glorious, I hope. I'm supposed to be despondent about the evil spell you've cast."

"Despondent yet determined," Jo said. "That's our Eliza." She glanced back at Hastings. As Dorinda chatted with the reverend, the director was gazing into the overhead rigging, no doubt checking to see that the lighting man on the catwalk was at the ready with his gas table, from which he could open and close valves that raised and dimmed the lights. Among the catwalks that ran through the rigging, his was the only one in use for this production.

Jo was grateful for that. There had been talk in the early rehearsals of having the Winter Witch descend to the stage from the fly rigging. But Hastings had decided that with a limited backstage crew, the effect would be more trouble than it was worth. For Jo, it was easier by far to step into the witch's role with both feet firmly planted on the ground.

Hastings raised his hand to the light man. The houselights dimmed. In the auditorium, the hum of conversation dissolved. The footlights came up, followed by the wing and border lights. Hands behind his back, Hastings strutted to center stage. With the booming voice of the retired actor that he was, he welcomed the theatregoers, then invited Reverent Worthington onstage to give the invocation.

To Jo's satisfaction, the reverend's words were brief and on point, making no mention of the aspects of the production that had so peeved him last night. In what amounted to a segue toward Dorinda's presentation, he asked a special blessing over the Hartfield Children's Home during this joyous time of year.

Dorinda was more long-winded with her remarks, as she was wont to be, but Hastings remained onstage with her, and he was able to gently prod her toward a conclusion. With that, the show was on.

Familiar as she was with how the plot unfolded, the presence of the audience electrified the air somehow, and Jo felt herself drawn into the show in a way that wasn't possible during rehearsals. It truly was a delightful plot, the magic of Christmas coming alive on the stage.

Before she knew it, the curtains were closing on Act One. As the stagehands raised and lowered the backdrops, she scurried onstage, positioning herself for the opening scene. The curtains opened, the border lights casting the Winter Witch's long shadow as she swept her arms about, invoking her power. "This Manor is mine, all mine," she cackled.

From there, Lord Mistletoe and Eliza took the stage, followed by Jingle and his forest sprites. As they departed, the Mouse crept from the corner, taking centerstage. Tilly had a small frame, and except for a shock of her red hair that had escaped from beneath the gray hood of her costume, she made an entirely believable mouse.

From the orchestra, the violins sounded a few mournful notes in a minor key. Tilly began to sing, the background hush deepening as the crystal notes of her song filled the air.

In the bleak midwinter
Frosty wind made moan
Earth stood hard as iron
Water like a stone
Snow had fallen
Snow on snow on snow
In the bleak midwinter
Long, long ago

She held the final note, then fell silent. What a gift, Jo thought, to be able to make such music.

Caught up as she was in the mood, Jo nearly missed her cue. The lights turned on her. Crouching, she rotated side to side, arms undulating, face contorted. "My spell shall never be broken!" Hubris at its finest.

The lights shifted stage right, and both Mouse Tilly and the Winter Witch retreated into the darkness. A discouraged Eliza took the stage, her mood reflecting the song's sentiment. Accompanied by his sprites, Jingle frolicked toward her, making his best attempt at cheer, but the despondent girl could not be comforted. All hope for joy at Mistletoe Manor seemed lost. The Winter Witch's hold was too strong.

In a rare sober moment, Jingle tried to comfort Eliza, who feared that without joy, her grandfather was losing his will to go on. Forest sprite Clara was the one who pointed them back to the enchanted book. The scene shifted to a dark forest where Eliza, guided by the enigmatic clues in the book, crept along a path in search of a castle where a powerful wizard resided. Hungry and thirsty, she came to a woodcutter's cottage.

With adamant gestures, Woodcutter Gus tried to turn her away. Bitter over his wife's death, he had spoken to no one in years. But Eliza would not be swayed, and the woodcutter broke down and shared the sustenance she required. Jingle urged her on to the castle, but Eliza's compassion for the woodcutter's plight prevailed. As he pantomimed his story, a single tear fell from her eyes.

The sprites, who'd been giggling over Jingle's frustration, fell silent. They looked on as Woodcutter Gus tipped Eliza's chin toward his face and wiped away her tear. At this moment, Jo noted a flash of envy in Sprite Felicity's eyes as Woodcutter Gus and his real-life love shared an impassioned stage kiss. But the audience couldn't tell. Collectively, they seemed to hold their breath. This was the real magic, Jo thought, being so drawn into a story that you scarcely remembered to breathe.

A yowl and the quick pattering of paws broke the tender moment. From stage right, the white alley cat dashed across the stage. Gripped tight in its jaws was a fish head. In hot pursuit, the black cat scampered after it, crashing into Amity's legs as it ran.

Gasps came from the audience, then titters of laughter as the cats chased one another in circles around the stage. "Mistletoe mischief!" someone yelled from the auditorium.

As Gus and Amity exchanged uncertain glances, the cat chase exited stage left. Its fishy treasure still in its mouth, the white cat nearly knocked over Jo, who was waiting in the wings. The putrid smell of rotting fish crept up from the hem of her robe.

Her cue hadn't come yet, but something had to be done to try to recover the scene. Striding onto the stage, she stepped in front of Gus and Amity, stealing the spotlight.

"Ruined! I'm ruined!" Jo cried as dramatically as she could manage. With a flourish, she sank in a heap to the floor, the skirt of her white robe puddling around her.

The drama of the Winter Witch's defeat seemed sufficient to pull the audience back into the story, and the theatrical proceeded without incident. The final scene arrived, the sleigh gliding from stage left to center stage along the tracks Noah had laid. Cleverly, he had cut back the strap of sleighbells so that the missing one wouldn't be noticed, and if the jingling was a little less robust than it had been in rehearsal, no one but the cast and crew knew it.

Gathering to join Mouse Tilly in the final sendoff, the actors exchanged glances, the memory of the cats' escapade still fresh in their minds. Then as Tilly led off, they joined in the singing.

Here we come a-Wassailing
Among the leaves so green
Here we come a wandering

So fairly to be seen
Love and joy come to you
And to you a Wassail too
God bless you and send you
A Happy New Year
God send you a Happy New Year

Applause resounded from the auditorium. The curtains closed. The stagehand who operated them glanced at Hastings. The director shook his head, signaling that there would be no reopening them, no matter the ovation. With two stray cats on the loose, tussling over a favorite meal, there was no sense tempting fate.

Gus rubbed his hand through his hair. "Well, that was unexpected. Seems the Mistletoe Magic got the best of us."

"You recovered for us beautifully, Jo," Amity said.

"It's what we witches do," Jo said.

"What I want to know is how they got in," Tilly said.

"And where they got that fish," Clara said.

"You have to admit, it did liven things up," Felicity said.

At the sharp sound of footsteps, they turned as one to see Dorinda Hamilton marching toward them like a soldier moving into battle position. Stopping before the actors, she glared from one cast member to the next. "These antics must not be allowed to continue. People paid to see a Christmas theatrical, not a circus."

"It wasn't intentional," Will said. "Even if it was rather amusing."

"Amusing?" Dorinda sputtered. "It could ruin my fundraiser. You think people are going to come tomorrow for a program featuring alley cats? I want to know who's responsible."

From the wings, Noah strode toward them. "I checked the back door. Someone had propped it open."

"To let in some air, maybe?" Wesley said. "It was stuffy backstage."

"Tomorrow night, I'll make sure it's secured," Noah said. "For now, we need to get this set broken down."

The cast and crew scattered, leaving Dorinda standing alone, center stage.

Chapter Six

When Jo arrived at the theatre the next night, the cats weren't the only ones waiting for her in the alley. Dorinda was there too. Jo didn't think she'd ever come upon her neighbor in a more unlikely spot.

"It smells back here." Dorinda crinkled her nose.

"You could have waited for the front doors to open."

"I wanted to see for myself where those cats came in."

As if they'd noted her disparaging tone, the cats slunk from behind the trash bin. One came up on either side of Jo to rub against her ankles. "Noah said he'd make sure the door was secured." Jo bent to pet the cats, each of them arching into her palm.

Dorinda drew back. "You're awfully cozy with those two," she said, her voice thick with suspicion.

"They're hungry. I bring them milk."

"And fish?"

"Please. You think I want to disrupt the theatrical?"

"Someone clearly does."

Jo wedged open the door, maneuvering her feet to block the cats from entering. "I'll be back in a minute with your bowl," she promised.

Dorinda slipped through the opening, and Jo followed behind her. Backstage, the sizzling anticipation of opening night was absent, the preparations for tonight's performance falling into something of a routine.

Jo started for the dressing area, but Dorinda stood in her path, hands on her hips.

"We need to get to the bottom of this," she said. "Someone deliberately sabotaged last night's performance, and with it, my orphans."

Jo suppressed a sigh. "We don't know that it was deliberate, Dorinda. Maybe someone was just careless with the door."

"Someone who also just happened to be carrying around a fish head? You know as well as I do that the salmon aren't running this time of year. And of everything I smelled in that alley, I detected no fish odor from the trash."

She had a point. Treating the cats to their milk last night, Jo didn't recall having smelled fish either.

"So it's a prank," Jo said. "A kid or something. They've had their fun. It won't happen again."

Dorinda looked pointedly around the backstage area. "I don't see any kids."

"Maybe one got in somehow. I don't know. Look, Dorinda. I have to get ready."

Dorinda stepped closer. "I'll tell you what I think." Her voice was low, her tone conspiratorial. "I think it was Felicity. I hear she wanted Amity's part as the lead. And from what I understand, she's been saying some not-so-nice things about her and Gus."

"People talk," Jo said. "They like to stir things up." Of all people, Dorinda should know.

"I was sitting in the front row last night. I saw the face she made when the love scene began. And you have to admit, she didn't look too upset with the cat hullabaloo. She looked like she was trying not to giggle."

"Maybe she's a little jealous of Amity. That doesn't mean she wants to ruin things."

"Well, I intend to find out, even if you don't. Felicity's right over there. I'm going to confront her with the evidence."

"Dorinda, please." Jo reached for her arm, but Dorinda pulled away, marching toward the dressing table where Felicity was applying her green forest sprite makeup.

For all her love of being the center of attention, Dorinda didn't participate in theatricals. She didn't understand how hard it could be to perform a role while upset. If she confronted Felicity head-on, they would likely have one very perturbed forest sprite on their hands. A forest sprite whom Jo had to admit did seem to bear a bit of a grudge already.

She hurried after Dorinda.

"Now, Felicity," she was saying as Jo arrived at the dressing table. "I know you wanted the lead in this production."

"Who wouldn't?" Felicity traced a thick line of green grease paint across her forehead. "Every girl in town would love to play alongside Gus Leighton."

"So a little mischief during the love scene makes perfect sense," Dorinda said.

"You're accusing me of luring in those cats?" Felicity dabbed grease paint on her cheeks. "That's ridiculous."

"Dorinda," Jo said. "This isn't the time or the place to be running around making wild accusations."

Dorinda paid her no mind. “All I’m saying, Felicity, is that if you took a more charitable attitude, we wouldn’t have to worry about any further incidents.”

Jo’s frustration boiled over. “You’re a fine one to lecture people on being charitable, Dorinda Hamilton. If I’d written down every mean-spirited comment I’ve heard you make, I’d have filled a whole book.”

Dorinda whirled toward her, eyes flashing. “I’ll admit I’ve said some uncharitable things in the past. But I don’t see why every off-handed remark I’ve ever made should be held against me. At least I don’t go around passing judgment like the high-and-mighty Jo Felch.”

With that, she stormed off.

“What got into her?” Felicity said.

“Worried about this charity business. If her efforts flop, she’ll think herself a failure, even if she’s loath to admit it.”

“I hope she gets it out of her head about me and those cats. Maybe I’m a little envious of Amity. Maybe I think I could have done a better job with the part. But that doesn’t mean I’m going to try and ruin the show. Even if I was so inclined, I’m allergic to cats. And did you get a whiff of that fish?”

Jo agreed that it was distasteful. Leaving Felicity to her makeup, she hurried off to get into costume herself. Transforming into the Winter Witch, she tried to put from her mind what Dorinda had said about her being judgmental. In her work as a reporter, she had to make all sorts of judgments. Nothing wrong with that, was there? Still, Dorinda’s high-and-mighty accusation kept coming back to her, even as she slipped out to feed the cats, making sure she closed the door firmly as she left them to lap up the milk.

When the lights dimmed and Dorinda came onstage to make her appeal, she seemed to have recovered her composure. If anything, she was more impassioned than she'd been the night before, evoking Dickens-worthy images of cold and starving orphans whose lives would be redeemed by the good graces of the people of Astoria.

What Reverend Worthington's invocation lacked in evocative imagery, he made up for with a sincere call for the magic onstage to move the audience to their own acts of love, joy, and gratitude. Perhaps watching the full performance last night, he'd seen its redemptive value.

If the thrill of opening night was over, it was offset by the assurance that came with having pulled off a successful performance, the cat chase aside. The few lines that the actors had stumbled over last night fell smoothly from their lips tonight. The set changes were flawless, and Noah had every prop in place.

Jo was certain she wasn't the only one holding her breath during tonight's love scene. But it went off without a hitch, the cats barred from entry. And this time, the transition to Jo's final line came as planned. Jingle made his pronouncement about love breaking the spell, and the lights shifted to where the Winter Witch stood.

"Ruined, I'm ruined!" Jo screeched.

A whoosh of wind went past her cheek. Pain shot through her shoulder, so sudden and severe that she crumpled to the stage. A thud resounded, the stage's wooden floor shuddering. Gasps came from the audience. From where she'd landed, Jo saw Noah in the wings, starting toward her.

She shook her head, warning him off. Thankfully, the lights man had the good sense to dim the lights that shone on her and instead, illuminate Jingle, who stood at the far corner of the stage, flanked by the forest sprites. Half-hobbling, half-crawling into the opposite wing, Jo glanced back, noting the alarm in their faces.

Recovering himself, Will launched into his lines, and the scripted action resumed. Noah reached for Jo. Gently, he pulled her close. "Are you all right?"

She nodded. "I – I think so." Instinctively, she reached with her opposite arm for her injured shoulder. She winced. "What was that?"

"A sandbag fell from the catwalk." Noah squinted at the darkened area overhead. "Ballast for the flying rigging." He shook his head. "The sandbags are roped to the catwalk. They shouldn't just fall like that."

"I think I preferred the cats." Gingerly, Jo rubbed her shoulder. "Far more entertaining."

"Come sit down." He guided her toward a closed trunk. "Catch your breath, and then we'll get you to Doc Vanderpool so he can have a look at that shoulder."

"No," she said, easing onto the trunk. "I'll be all right. I can move my arm." She demonstrated, making a feeble up and down motion that increased her pain only a little. "It's probably just a bad bruise. Scared me, that's all."

"Knocked you off your feet."

"At least the timing was right. The Witch defeated."

He frowned. "A little too convenient, I'd say."

"You think someone messed with the rigging."

"I don't know what else would explain it. Those sandbags can't untie themselves from their ropes."

"What about Felicity?" Jo said. "Where was she when the sandbag fell?"

He looked at her quizzically. “On the far side of the stage, getting ready to come out with Clara and Will. What does she have to do with anything?”

“Nothing, I expect. Dorinda met me at the backstage door tonight, all wound up about those cats last night. Before I could stop her, she was laying into Felicity about sabotaging the show because she resents not getting the lead role. Felicity took it better than I thought she would, but Dorinda stomped off, angry at me for rebuking her.”

“No offense to Felicity, but I don’t think she’s agile enough to be climbing around in the rigging.”

“I expect you’re right.” When the rest of them were young and climbing trees, Felicity had always kept her feet firmly on the ground.

“You’re sure you’re okay?” Even in the darkened backstage area, she could see the concern in his eyes.

“I’ll be fine. You’d best retrieve that sandbag before some-one trips over it. I’ll sit here and figure out how to deal with Dorinda. It might be my shoulder that’s hurt, but I guarantee she’ll be taking personal affront at another disruption to the show.”

CHAPTER SEVEN

In the way of most injuries, Jo's shoulder hurt more the next day than it had right after the sandbag glanced off it. Waking the next morning, she saw that a big purple bruise had spread over her shoulder, making her glad that neither the Winter Witch's robe nor her pretty red Christmas dress had off-the-shoulder sleeves.

At least it was her left shoulder that was hurt, making it relatively easy to hide her limited mobility in that arm from her father. With the way word spread around town, he'd find out soon enough, but in the meantime, she didn't want him to worry, or worse yet, try to dissuade her from performing tonight. Fannie's mother had sent word that she was still abed and would be doing well to be up by Christmas.

At the newspaper office, Jo discovered that typing wasn't easy with an injured shoulder. Tackling the Christmas Eve church notices, some delivered in scrawled handwriting she could scarcely make out, pain shot down her arm whenever she stretched the fingers of her left hand to plunk on a typewriter key.

At her desk, Amity looked up from the wire stories she was scanning. "Enough of that." Standing, she came over to where Jo sat. "You look as if every letter you type is a struggle."

"Not every letter. The e's and r's, mostly."

"Get up," Amity said. "We're trading places. You're better with the wire stories anyhow."

"I'm just glad that thing didn't hit me in the head." Jo started to get up and cede her spot to Amity, but just then, the front door swung open.

On a blast of cold air, Dorinda burst into the office. "I thought you'd be home in bed." She strode straight for Jo's desk, peeling off her gloves as she went. "I couldn't believe it when Effie told me you'd gone to *work.*" This last word she said as if it were some sort of wicked affliction cast upon sinners as punishment.

"It's only my shoulder that hurts."

"Only your shoulder." Dorinda sank into the chair beside Jo's desk. "Do you realize how serious it could have been? A sandbag, falling from that height?"

"We were just discussing that," Amity said.

"I tried telling Jo last night," Dorinda said. "Someone has it in for that production. And now my charity cause is being dragged down with it. We've got to put a stop to these mishaps before anyone else gets hurt."

"You're proposing the rest of the performances be canceled?" Jo asked.

"Of course not. We mustn't give the saboteur the satisfaction. We must root him out."

"Or her," Amity said.

"To that point, it can't have been Felicity," Jo said. "Noah pointed out that she's not agile enough to go climbing around in the rigging."

"What about Reverend Worthington?" Amity said. "He's older, but he's spry. Played football or some such thing when he was younger, as I recall."

"But he's a man of the cloth," Dorinda said. "Why ever would you suspect him?"

"He came around during one of our rehearsals, demanding the production be shut down," Jo said. "He thinks it's frivolous."

"And he feared it would detract from his church's Christmas Eve pageant," Amity said.

"Nevertheless, he gives an enthusiastic invocation," Dorinda said. "And I sat near him in the front row. He applauded heartily, as I recall."

"So he stayed until the performance ended last night?" Amity asked.

Dorinda's lips turned in a small frown. "Now that you mention it, he left at the end of Act One."

"He dresses all in black," Amity said. "So he could have gone backstage and climbed up into the catwalks without anyone noticing."

"But how would he know there were sandbags up there?" Jo asked. "It's not as if he's spent a lot of time behind the scenes at the Opera House."

"Maybe he didn't know," Dorinda said. "Maybe he went looking around and spied them."

Jo shook her head. "I just can't see him doing something that could have injured someone."

"The intent might not have been to hurt anyone," Amity said. "Only to shake things up."

"You heard what Noah said last night after he climbed up there to have a look around," Jo said. "A rope was cut. That seems intentional."

"Cut and frayed," Amity said. "Like someone thought they could control the sandbag's falling but misjudged its weight."

"Which would mean they weren't out to kill you, Jo." Dorinda spoke as if to reassure her, but it had rather the opposite effect, bringing forward the notion that the potentially lethal missile had been aimed at Jo.

"First the book and the sleighbell," Jo said. "Then the cats. Now the falling sandbag. It's as if someone is trying harder and harder to make some sort of point."

"The book and the sleighbell?" Dorinda repeated. She looked puzzled.

"The enchanted book," Jo said. "Noah put a great deal of effort into making it look just right for the show, and then it went missing. He searched high and low. Finally, he gave up and substituted another prop."

"What about the sleighbell?" Amity said. "I don't remember anything being said about that."

"That same night, Noah discovered a sleighbell missing from the sleigh that's used in Act Three. Not a huge loss since there are other bells on the strip. But puzzling all the same."

"Let's assume the same person is behind all of it," Dorinda said.

"Person or persons," Amity said. "There could be more than one involved."

"True," Dorinda conceded. "We have the missing book and sleighbell. We have a back door propped open and two stray cats lured inside with a stinky piece of fish. We have a sandbag released from the rigging. All on different nights. We need to determine who was there for all those events."

"Pretty much the whole cast and crew," Jo said. "Except Fannie."

"The crew," Dorinda said. "Who would that be?"

"Hank and Albert," Amity said. "They change the backdrops and operate the curtains."

"Christian," Jo said. "He runs the lights. And Noah, of course. He oversees the crew. But he swears they were all accounted for when the sandbag fell."

"The lights man," Dorinda said. "He's up high, isn't he? In those...what do you call them?"

"Catwalks," Amity said. "Noah talked with him after the show ended. He was pretty shook up about what happened. Said he thought he'd heard a shifting of some sort up there before the bag fell, but he didn't think much of it. He felt terrible that he hadn't investigated."

"He certainly should have." Dorinda spoke with such indignation that one might have thought she was the injured actor, not Jo.

"Working the lights takes a great deal of concentration," Jo said. "Lots of cues to attend to. If the lighting is off, it fouls everything up."

"Hard to see how things could be in more disarray than they are now," Dorinda said glumly. "What about access to the catwalk? Would that make anyone more suspect than the rest?"

"It's by a narrow set of stairs to the left of the stage," Amity said. "Not especially well lit, so a person has to be a little like a cat to negotiate them, not to mention climbing around while they're up there."

"Who would have been in that area prior to your going out on stage, Jo?" Dorinda asked.

"Immediately prior? All I remember is Noah. And Mr. Hastings. But he left to check on a problem Wesley was having with his costume."

"Mr. Hastings," Dorinda said. "That's intriguing."

"It's his show," Jo said. "He wouldn't sabotage it."

"You never know," Dorinda said. "Maybe he's secretly disappointed in how it turned out, and he wants an excuse not to shut it down."

"He wouldn't need an excuse," Amity said. "He's the director. He could just cancel the last two performances."

"Which he hasn't done," Jo said. "Despite everything that's happened. Look, Dorinda. I appreciate your wanting to get to the bottom of this, but I feel as if we're getting rather far-fetched with these theories. Maybe this is the end of it. Maybe tonight, everything will go off without a hitch."

Interrupting their speculations, a messenger boy burst into the office. "From Reverend Worthington." The boy offered the folded note in his hand, looking from one woman to the next, seeming uncertain about who should receive it.

Jo took it from him, and the boy scurried off.

Unfolding the paper, she scanned what the reverend had written in his flowing script. "Miss Hartfield will receive you at 11 o'clock tomorrow morning to discuss the matter of her attendance on behalf of the Children's Home."

"Miss Cordelia Hartfield?" Dorinda asked. "Founder of the Hartfield Children's Home?"

"The very same," Jo said. "Reverend Worthington told me that with her health declining, she has retired to Astoria and is a member of his church, though due to her health, she only occasionally attends services."

"But no one told me," Dorinda said, her feathers ruffled.

"I was waiting to hear whether she would consent to attending the final performance. I thought you might pay tribute to her from the stage when you speak about your charity drive."

Dorinda took a second to process this request. "That would be a splendid addition to my appeal."

"And a nice item for the paper to cover," Amity said.

"That's the purpose of my meeting with her tomorrow," Jo said. "I'm hoping she'll share a few of her experiences for us to publish in the paper. If she consents to attending the final performance, someone will need to help her get there. Can you do that, Dorinda?"

"Certainly," Dorinda said. "I'll call for her in Father's carriage. At half past six." She leaned to see the address on Reverend Worthington's note. "No, a quarter past. I'll have Warren come along in case—"

"Before you make too many plans," Jo interrupted, "I need to confirm that she's willing to attend. I'll send word after I meet with her tomorrow."

Dorinda stood. "Good. Just don't get hit by another sandbag between now and then."

Chapter Eight

Happily, the third night of the show went off without a hitch, unless one was to count Wesley tripping over his cane in Act One, which he readily admitted was his own fault for shuffling along without paying proper attention to his feet. When the curtain closed on the final act, the cast and crew were in high spirits. Whatever forces had conspired against them, they seemed to have been allayed. A celebratory mood prevailed. They had only one more night to get through.

If not for the pain in her shoulder, Jo could almost forget that anything had gone awry. Walking her home from the Opera House, Noah urged her again to let the doctor have a look. She assured him that it was no worse than the time when she'd fallen from a tree limb, scrambling to keep up with him and Amity when they were children.

Stopping just beyond the flickering glow of a gas lamp, she drew him into a kiss, telling him it was the least he could do to make it up to her. Assuring her he could do much more, he returned the kiss with a passion that all but erased her pain, at least for the moment.

With the December days growing short, Jo left the house the next morning just as the sun was casting its first feeble light through the mist hovering over Astoria's rooftops. Wisps of chimney smoke curled in the frigid air, merging with the gray.

Stepping from the grand porch of her father's house, she breathed in the sharp scent of pine from the trees that towered over the hillside. From the river below, the cries of circling gulls pierced the quiet of a town that had yet to fully rouse itself to meet the demands of the day. As a passing riverboat blasted its steam whistle, Jo hugged her coat close, her breath hanging in the air.

As she started down the frosty cobblestone pathway, her boot slipped. Catching her balance, she glanced up at the clouds. If the temperatures continued their plunge, Astoria's usual winter rain might well turn to snow. Last January, snow had fallen during a similar cold spell. With Noah and their friends, she'd gone down to Clatsop by horse-drawn sleigh, bells jingling all the way, to skate on the lakes. Coming home after dark, she and Noah had crept down to the cellar to retrieve her father's old sled. With much effort and muffled laughter, they'd dragged it outside and up the hill for a slide.

Smiling at this memory, she heard her name being called.

"Jo!" Coming from next door, Dorinda hurried over the cobblestones toward her.

"Careful," Jo said. "It's slipperier than it looks."

Bundled in her fur coat, Dorinda slowed her approach. "You'll never guess what I found out."

"It must be important. I don't recall you ever being out so early in the day."

Coming close, Dorinda's visible puffs of breath mingled with Jo's. "Oh, it's important, believe me. You see, the Flavel girls have been simply begging me to stop by their house, so I didn't stay for the show after my introductory remarks last night. Were there any mishaps?"

"None at all," Jo said. "Perhaps we've seen the last of it."

"I doubt it. Not after what I've learned. There was quite a gathering there at the Flavels. Polly, Violet, Lila, Grace." Dorinda ticked off the names on her gloved fingers. "Floretta, Marge, Caroline, Maude. Plus Nellie and Katie, of course. Oh, and they served the most delightful little sandwiches, some sort of mayonnaise salad with ham. I must see if Cook can get the recipe."

Cold seeping through her boots, Jo stamped her feet, right, left, right. "Sounds delicious. But if that's all—"

"Of course it's not all." Looking affronted, Dorinda drew herself up. "There was the usual music, of course. Christmas carols on the harp and dulcimer. And that led to singing. Do you have any idea how many verses there are to 'The First Noel'?"

"Not really. But I'm missing the connection here with the theatrical."

"Why, the singing, of course. We girls got to talking about who in Astoria has the sweetest voice, and naturally I mentioned Tilly from the theatrical. Several others agreed that her singing ability is exceptional. That's when Marge filled us in on Tilly's background. She was raised at the Hartfield Children's Home. Can you believe it? I had no idea."

"Nor did I."

"Don't you find it odd that she failed to mention that to me? She knows what I'm doing to raise money for the Home. She could have joined me on stage to encourage donations. But she hasn't said a peep."

“She hasn’t been in Astoria all that long. Perhaps she didn’t want to presume.”

“Or perhaps she holds a grudge against the Children’s Home, and she’s sabotaging the theatrical to ruin my charity effort.”

“That seems a little extreme, don’t you think?”

“You have a better idea?”

“I do. Take last night’s uneventful performance as a good sign and carry on. Let bygones be bygones.”

“And risk someone else getting hurt? Think about it, Jo. What do we really know about Tilly O’Malley?”

“We know that her husband works as a manager at the mill, and that they came here from Portland. We know that she sings like an angel. And now we have this coincidence of her having lived at the Children’s Home. That hardly makes her suspect.”

“But don’t you see? Maybe she doesn’t like the idea of me raising money for the home. Maybe she wishes she’d have thought of it first, seeing as how she grew up there.”

“I truly can’t see Tilly O’Malley getting upset about something like that.”

“I don’t see that you’ve come up with any more likely suspects.”

“Nor do I see the need to.”

“So you’re just going to stand out there like a sitting duck and pray something else doesn’t come flying at you from the rafters.”

“The catwalks.” Jo refrained from correcting her sitting-standing discrepancy. “I’ve got to get going, Dorinda. I’ve the paper to tend to. Not to mention my feet are freezing.” She started down the pathway.

"Very well," Dorinda called after her. "I can see that you're leaving this all up to me. I shall have a word with Tilly myself. I know where she lives."

Jo whirled around. "You intend to go to her house and confront her?"

"Better than confronting her right before she goes onstage to sing."

When Dorinda got an idea in her head, she could be like a runaway train. The only way to dissuade her was to divert her energy.

"All right, Dorinda. I see you're not going to let this go. I'll help with your inquiries." Otherwise, Jo thought, Dorinda's inquiries might so offend Tilly that she wouldn't show up for the final performance. "But first, we need to gather some information. How about you come along with me to speak with Cordelia Hartfield this morning? If this rumor about Tilly is true, Miss Hartfield will remember her, and she may have some counsel as to how to approach her with your concerns. If the rumor proves false, there's no need to confront Tilly. Either way, your presence might encourage Miss Hartfield to attend tonight's performance."

"Marvelous!" Dorinda pressed her gloved hands together beneath her chin. Behind all her bluster, it struck Jo that what she wanted above all else was to be included. Setting herself above the rest of the town, she might be lonelier than Jo had thought. "I'll fetch you in Father's carriage at a quarter till eleven."

With the wintery chill in the air this morning, a ride in the town's finest carriage was not something Jo was about to turn down. "Very well. A quarter till eleven."

At the newspaper office, the morning passed quickly. As was their usual practice, Jo worked with Amity to layout the first two pages. Containing less timely material—and thankfully for the newspaper's ever precarious balance sheet, plenty of advertisements—the remaining pages were already set. Debating over which wire stories should make the cut to make room for the article Jo hoped to write about Miss Hartfield, they finished the layouts just as the typesetter, Nan, arrived. Complaining of the cold, she hung her wrap and got to work with her compositor's stick.

Moments later, Jo saw through the plate glass window that the Hamilton carriage was slowing to a stop in front of the office. "Wish me luck," she said, having explained to Amity her plan to prevent Dorinda's upsetting Tilly with unfounded accusations.

"Hopefully, Miss Hartfield will prove an ally," Amity said. "Rather than adding fuel to the fire."

"I can't imagine her doing that." Jo fastened the buttons of her woolen coat. "Mr. Hastings could scarcely have cast a more perfect person for the Mouse than Tilly. How Dorinda came up with this notion of her disrupting the theatrical is beyond me."

"It's Dorinda," Amity said. "I just hope you're able to dissuade her from confronting Tilly. Even a Mouse has her limits. The last thing we need is to have her refuse to show up tonight because she's affronted at being accused. Without her singing, Mistletoe Manor would be missing a lot of its magic."

"I'll do my best," Jo said.

If anything, the air outside was crisper than it had been earlier in the day, the blanket of clouds overhead threatening snow. As the coachman helped Jo into the carriage, she was enveloped by warmth emanating from the footwarmers beneath the seats, heightening the scent of aging leather and polished wood.

"Look at us." In the plush velvet seat across from where Jo sat, Dorinda looked resplendent in her fur seal coat, her burgundy gown peeking out from beneath the coat's bottom edge. A matching sealskin muff concealed her hands. "Headed to solve a mystery together."

"Let's not presume too much," Jo said. "And it would be best if you allowed me to guide the conversation, Dorinda. Miss Hartfield agreed to an interview, not an interrogation."

"Fine," Dorinda said, in a tone that said it was anything but fine. "You're the one who makes all the character judgments anyhow."

Jo resisted the urge to point out that character judgments were part of the news business. If Dorinda chose to feel judged, that was her problem.

With a rhythmic clip-clop of the horses' hooves, the carriage set off, the wooden street planks rumbled beneath. Stealing glances through the carriage's frosty window, Jo took in the downtown buildings decked out in holiday cheer. Garlands of evergreens graced the stately arched windows of the First Astoria Bank. On the door of Mabel Parker's seamstress shop hung a wreath woven through with brightly colored silk ribbons. In Stanley Osborne's dry goods store, a Christmas tree festooned with paper chains and cranberries filled the window display.

As the horses trotted up the hill to the residential district, Jo broke the icy tension between her and Dorinda by asking about how the Hamilton household was faring in Gladys Hamilton's absence. This set off a round of chatter from Dorinda about the troubles her mother had written about in her letters, her sister's illness and the less than luxurious accommodations she was forced to endure in the rough-and-tumble outpost of Seattle. Nodding along and asking an occasional question, Jo hoped that this diversion would not erase from Dorinda's mind the protocols she'd laid out, that Jo was to guide the interview with Miss Hartfield.

The carriage stopped outside a modest home on a quiet side street. As the coachman helped her and Dorinda down the carriage steps, Jo noted the home's faded white façade, weathered by the region's many storms. As Dorinda instructed the coachman to wait, Jo fished her calling card from her reticule.

Side by side, she and Dorinda proceeded up the narrow walkway to the porch, its wooden steps creaking as they ascended. "How tragic," Dorinda murmured. "A life devoted to service, and this is her reward."

More than tragedy, Jo sensed a quiet dignity here. A simple wreath of pine and holly adorned the front door, and delicate lace curtains covered the front windows. She rapped sharply on the door, mindful that Miss Hartfield might be hard of hearing, then waited with Dorinda until the door swung open, revealing a woman who was stooped with age, her gray hair pulled back in a severe bun. She looked them up and down with an intensity in her pale blue eyes that Jo found disarming.

"Miss Hartfield?" She presented her card. "I'm Josephine Felch, from the *Astoria Evening Register*. Reverend Worthington said I might call today at eleven to discuss your role at the Children's Home."

Miss Hartfield nodded slightly, which Jo took as encouragement to go on.

"And this is Dorinda Hamilton," Jo said. "She has been raising money for the Children's Home this holiday season.

I believe Reverend Hamilton mentioned that a portion of the proceeds from the town's Christmas theatrical will benefit Dorinda's project. She would be most pleased if you made an appearance at the show tonight."

"A pleasure to meet you, Miss Hartfield." Dorinda handed over her own calling card. "I am so impressed at how you devoted your life to helping the orphans."

Breaking the lines that seemed to turn her lips downward. Miss Hartfield offered a tentative smile. "How kind of you to say so. Please, come in."

A bit unsteadily, Miss Hartfield stepped back from the door. A faint mustiness tickled Jo's nostrils as she stepped inside, followed by Dorinda.

"Follow me." Despite a gravelly quaver in her voice, the elderly woman spoke firmly. Turning, she led them toward an open doorway. Clad in a modest gray dress, she moved with slow, deliberate steps.

As they entered the front room, Dorinda's eyes widened, taking in the threadbare rug and the aging rocking chair. In the small fireplace, a paltry blaze struggled to cast off the chill. Perched on the fireplace mantle was a framed photograph of a younger Cordelia, surrounded by a group of children, their sober gazes frozen in time. Alongside it, as well as on the end tables, was an assortment of other memorabilia that looked to be associated with the Children's Home.

"May I take your wraps?" Miss Hartfield asked.

Dorinda glanced at Jo, uncertainty in her eyes.

"Thank you, but we can't stay long," Jo said, unbuttoning her coat but leaving it on.

"Then I won't offer you tea." Miss Hartfield seemed relieved. "Please, have a seat."

Settling on a loveseat that must have once been a delightful shade of mauve but had since faded to the color of a drooping rose, Jo sat by necessity closer to Dorinda than she had since they were children. Easing herself into the rocking chair, Miss Hartfield seemed to shrink in stature, her stopped shoulders at odds with her head, which she held high.

"As Reverend Worthington no doubt explained, we'd like to run a short piece in the newspaper about your founding of the Children's Home," Jo said, taking her pencil and notepad from her reticule. "I don't think many people in Astoria know that you're here."

"Which suits me fine." Miss Hartfield clasped her hands in her lap, perhaps to stop the trembling in her fingers. "As one gets older, one realizes that notoriety takes many forms, not all of them desirable."

"Oh, but you did such a service, taking in those poor orphans," Dorinda said.

"You mustn't make me out to be a saint, dear." Despite her physical decline, Miss Hartfield's tone carried an air of authority. "In the most charitable terms, one might say my devotion to those children was a distraction. Less favorably, it might be deemed an act of self-interest to quell my own grief. You see, I lost my dear husband and our two precious children coming over the Oregon Trail."

Jo jotted a note. "Where did you come from?"

"Illinois. My husband was an ambitious man. He worked his family's farm, and that provided well enough for us. But the temptation of mild winters and rich soils in the Willamette Valley proved too great for him. And land free for the taking—we could scarcely imagine it." She paused, a faraway look in her eyes. "I was skeptical about traveling so far from home, as you might imagine. But I wasn't about to be one of those wives who stayed behind."

"What year was this?" Jo asked, looking up from her notes.

"We made our decision to leave in 1854. The following year we set out. I'll spare you the details of the hardships we encountered. Suffice to say there were many. We buried our son, Prentice, in Kansas. Struck with cholera one day, dead the next. Our daughter, Francis, made Nebraska before cholera took her too. They were best of friends, my darling children. I don't think she had the will to go on. Our hearts were broken. I begged Evan to turn back, so that at least we might grieve our losses with the comfort of family and friends. But he wouldn't hear of it. Determined, he was. When he latched onto some idea or another, you couldn't persuade him to let go of it."

"Such hardship." Dorinda seemed visibly moved. "I can't imagine."

The bowed legs of Miss Hartfield's chair creaked against the wooden floor as she rocked gently forward and back, forward and back. "In Wyoming, Indians attacked our camp, stealing oxen and horses. The men assembled a posse to retrieve them. Naturally, Evan insisted on going along. Things got out of hand. Our men killed five of the Indians. The Indians killed three of our men, including my Evan. My sorrow was beyond what I thought I could bear. But at that point, I could scarcely turn back alone. A kindly doctor stepped in to drive my wagon. Two days after I buried Evan, a woman from another wagon died in childbirth. The doctor asked me to care for her baby. The simple act of tending that child helped me go on. When we reached Oregon, the babe's aunt took her. But I knew there were hundreds of other orphaned children who had no family waiting for them here. So I drew from what little strength was left to me and raised money to build the Children's Home."

"That's a remarkable achievement," Jo said. "What made you choose Weston instead of Portland as the location?"

The wistful look Jo had noted earlier returned to the former matron's eyes. "I was reaching for the memories of happier days, I suppose. Portland was already growing, and I couldn't see how all the fumes spewing from those smokestacks could be good for children. And back in Illinois, Francis and Prentice had so loved playing along the banks of the Spoon River. When I found a piece of property along the river outside of Weston, those memories came flooding back. Fresh air to breathe, frogs to catch, trees to climb. Not that the Columbia turned out to be anything like that muddy old Spoon River." She touched her fingers to her weathered face. "Half these wrinkles came from my worry over the children falling into the river and getting swept away."

"But they had their fresh air and trees." Dorinda seemed captivated by Miss Hartfield's story. "How did you manage them all? I understand that at its peak, you had twenty-six children there."

Jo jotted down this number. Dorinda did seem as if she knew a fair amount about her pet charity project.

"Not all that well, I'm afraid. Oh, at the time, I thought I was doing a fine job with the children. Kept order, established routines. But now that I've stepped away, I have my regrets." She turned to Jo. Despite her frailty, there was a glimmer of fierce determination in her eyes. "That is all I care to say. I presume it's enough for your little article?"

"I – I suppose," Jo said, caught off-guard. She closed her notepad and slipped it back into her reticule, along with her pencil.

"But she hasn't told us about Tilly," Dorinda said.

"Tilly?" Miss Hartfield tipped her head quizzically.

Jo considered the quickest way around the topic, enough to satisfy Dorinda without prying into Tilly's past. "I suppose you've come across your charges now and then, long after they've left your care. Dorinda learned recently that Tilly O'Malley may have grown up at the Children's Home."

"She did grow up there," Dorinda said crossly. "That's what I was told."

"Tilly O'Malley," Miss Hartfield repeated. "I don't recall a child by that name."

"Perhaps it was another Children's Home she was raised in," Jo said.

"No," Dorinda insisted. "Marge was quite clear. Tilly grew up in Hartfield Children's Home. But her name wouldn't have been O'Malley. That's her married name. Her husband is the new manager at the mill."

"No matter." Jo noted the weariness in Miss Hartfield's eyes. "It was only a small coincidence. Tilly has the singing part in our Christmas production, the one that's tied to Dorinda's charity effort."

Miss Hartfield raised an eyebrow. "A petite little redhead?"

"Yes," Dorinda said, giving Jo a pointed look. "Tilly's small, and she has red hair."

"Oh, but that would be Matilda. Matilda Dunaway. A great one for singing she was. Voice like a lark, and with a little bird's energy too. Always flitting here and there, making mischief. Such a time I had keeping up with her."

"Mischief," Dorinda said. "You mean she played pranks?"

"All sorts of pranks. Switching salt and sugar in the kitchen. Ringing the dinner bell in the middle of the night and waking us all. And she ran off so many times, I lost count. I'd find her hiding under the back porch, her skirt covered in dirt. Or up in a tree. A great one for climbing, she was."

"Climbing," Dorinda repeated, giving Jo another knowing look. "Last you knew, what was she up to?"

"I couldn't say. As she got older, she'd run farther and farther away. I'd have to summon the Weston constable, and he'd drag her back from town, kicking and screaming. Finally, when she was sixteen, I quit trying to find her. Naturally, I feared what fate might have befallen her." Miss Hartfield pressed her hand to her chest. "After all these years, it would do my heart good to know she'd made a happy life for herself."

Dorinda clapped her hands together. "How perfect! When you come to the program tonight, you two can catch up with each other."

"I don't know." Miss Hartfield glanced at the window, then back at Dorinda. "I'm too tired these days to go out in the evenings."

"Then we'll leave now, so you can get some rest." Dorinda jumped up from the loveseat.

"If Miss Hartfield says she's too tired to attend, we need to respect that," Jo said, rising more slowly than Dorinda had.

"You'll be ready, won't you, Miss Hartfield?" Dorinda said, ignoring Jo's remark. "I'll be back to fetch you in the carriage at a quarter past six. I'll point you out to the audience, and you can say a few words if you like. Or just give a little wave if that's all you're feeling up to. It will mean a great deal to everyone who turns out to support the Children's Home. And to watch the show," she added, almost as an afterthought.

"It is a worthy cause," Miss Hartfield said hesitantly. "Despite everything."

"Then it's settled." Dorinda gestured toward the door. "Come along," she said, as if Jo had been dawdling. "You've got an article to write."

Chapter Nine

As they left Cordelia Hartfield's house, Jo did her best to dissuade Dorinda from her plans. Pushing Miss Hartfield into attending tonight's show was a bad idea, she pointed out, considering not only her age but the uneasiness with which she'd spoken of her experiences.

To this, Dorinda replied that Cordelia's attending the show had been Jo's idea in the first place, and if she was going to use the Children's Home connection to placate Reverend Worthington, the least she could do was not stand in the way of its former matron making an appearance tonight.

Jo conceded the point about the reverend, but when Dorinda launched into speculation about Tilly O'Malley, Jo shut her down. Confirming that Tilly had indeed grown up at the Children's Home didn't mean that she'd been behind the trouble at the theatrical, she told Dorinda in the most uncertain terms she could muster.

With that, Jo folded her arms across her chest and did her best to ignore Dorinda's ramblings. Finally, the carriage wheels slowed. Jo rubbed her fisted hand over the window, melting a circle in the frost. Instead of the clapboard building that housed the *Evening Register,* she looked out on the sprawling complex of barn-red buildings that made up the Astoria Lumber Mill.

"Your coachman has made a mistake," she said. "This isn't my office."

"It's not a mistake." Dorinda offered a sly, satisfied smile. "I instructed him to bring us here upon leaving Miss Hartfield's house. We're going to pay Tilly a visit."

"We most certainly are not," Jo said. "Tell him to take me back to my office immediately."

"We won't be long."

"Long isn't the problem," Jo said. "The problem is accosting Tilly with innuendos."

The coachman opened the carriage door, letting in a blast of cold air laced with the piney smell of cut timber. Rising from her seat, Dorinda ducked through the opening. "If you're going to be stubborn about it, you can wait here. I'm going to have a chat with her."

A chain of disasters flashed through Jo's mind. Tilly's horror at being confronted with mischief in which she'd had no part, followed by her refusal to sing tonight, followed by the whole production falling apart.

Gathering her skirt, she followed Dorinda out of the carriage and onto the walkway. If she couldn't stop her, she could at least try to mitigate the damage.

As they started up the boardwalk, Jo made a last pass at reason. "You have absolutely no evidence that Tilly has done anything other than put on her mouse costume and sing," she said.

"You heard Miss Hartfield," Dorinda said, speaking over the distant whine of a saw from the mill. "Tilly played pranks as a child. She climbed trees."

"As did I," Jo said. "Although Noah outdid me with the pranks. I don't see you accusing either of us."

"She grew up in an orphanage," Dorinda said, as if that explained everything.

The house they approached was part of a complex of company housing on the east end of the sprawling Astoria Lumber Mill property. Its peaked roof stood taller than the other structures, but it had the same shingles, the same barn-red exterior paint. Next to the front door, someone had planted a leggy rose bush, a single shriveled bloom still clinging to its stem despite the frost.

To Jo's relief, there was no response to Dorinda's knock. "Tilly's not home." She tugged at Dorinda's sleeve. "Let's go."

But Dorinda stood firm. A moment later, the door swung open. Tilly O'Malley stood before them, her red hair loosely tied back with a white ribbon. Wearing a white apron over a pale green dress, she seemed a different person than the small woman in the gray mouse suit. Flour smudged her nose, and the pleasant smell of ginger wafted from the kitchen.

Surprise showed in her eyes as she looked from Jo to Dorinda and back again. Dorinda offered her card. "Dorinda Hamilton. You've seen me at the theatrical, I expect. I'm the one raising funds for the Children's Home."

"Yes." Taking the card, Tilly shoved it into her apron pocket. "I'm afraid I can't receive visitors now. I'm making gingerbread men to give to the millworkers' children."

"What a lovely gesture," Dorinda said. "We won't mind accompanying you to the kitchen, will we, Jo?"

"We shan't bother you." Jo reached for Dorinda's arm. "Come along, Dorinda. You can speak with Tilly after tonight's performance."

Shrugging from Jo's reach, Dorinda edged toward Tilly, causing her to take a step back. "After the performance will be too late. You see, we have a special guest in mind for tonight. An important person from your past."

A look of alarm flashed across Tilly's face. Then her composure returned. "Who might that be?"

Dorinda sniffed the air. "Your cookies. I hope they're not burning."

Tilly twisted her head toward the kitchen, visible through an open doorway. "Excuse me, please. I'll be right back." She hurried toward the kitchen.

"Dorinda, I really think..."

But Dorinda was already halfway to the kitchen. There was nothing to do but follow.

The kitchen was warm, smelling not just of ginger but also of molasses and cinnamon. Grabbing a hot pad, Tilly opened the oven door and pulled out a metal sheet containing six good-sized gingerbread men, a bit dark at the edges but otherwise unscathed. As she set the cookie sheet aside to cool, Dorinda pulled out a chair. Atop the table were platters of baked gingerbread men stacked three deep.

Tilly turned. "I'd offer you a seat, but I see you've already found one." Her tone was mostly one of resignation, but Jo also detected a hint of bitterness. "Miss Felch, you may as well have a seat too. I'll just be a moment."

Feeling every bit the intruder, Jo sat across the table from Dorinda. With the two of them looking on, Tilly expertly maneuvered her floured spatula, loosening bits of dough as she lifted six more gingerbread men from the countertop to an empty metal sheet. Also on the counter were canisters marked *Flour* and *Sugar*, as well as a recipe book opened to a page smudged with what looked molasses.

Tilly tucked the new batch of cookies inside the oven, wiped her hands on a towel, and sat down at the table between them. "Ten minutes. That's all I've got. I need to get these gingerbread men frosted to distribute when the men get off work."

"I'll get straight to the point," Dorinda said. "I understand you grew up at the Hartfield Children's Home."

Surprise showed in Tilly's face. "Who told you that?"

"A friend," Dorinda said. "I assume it's no secret."

"I suppose it isn't," she said. "I've told my husband countless times that I'd rather people not know, but he seems to find it a badge of honor, his little wife who survived her upbringing in an orphanage."

"Your experience was unhappy?" Dorinda said.

"Tilly, there's no need to talk about it if you don't want to. Dorinda and I can be on our way." Jo gave Dorinda a pointed stare.

Tilly looked squarely at Dorinda, something in her expression hardening. "I understand that the orphanage is your little pet project. But as far as I'm concerned, that place should be shut down. Do you have any idea was it's like to be at the mercy of someone else's supposed benevolence? Someone who favors every other child living there over you?"

"But Cordelia Hartfield—" Dorinda began.

"Cordelia Hartfield hated me. I admit, I wasn't the easiest child. Try as I might, I couldn't recall my parents. I was orphaned when I was two. All I wanted was for someone to pay attention to me, for someone to hold me and tell me I was worth loving even when I misbehaved." A tear rolled down her cheek. She wiped it away with her hand. "Instead, I got, 'Stand up straight, Matilda' and 'Quit running, Matilda' and 'One more prank, and you'll sit in the corner all weekend.'"

Jo touched her hand. "That must have been hard for you."

"When people donated clothing and shoes for us—we lived on hand-me-downs, you know—the other girls got first pick, and I got what was left over. The ugly dress, the too-big shoes. When the matron organized outings, I got left behind. I was too wild, she said. Too untamed."

Tilly wiped away another tear. "I hated Christmas. Miss Hartfield chose her favorites to perform in a special holiday program. All the big donors attended. She knew I could sing. But she never let me."

"With your beautiful voice." Dorinda looked as if she herself might be moved to tears.

"You can't imagine how thrilled I was when Mr. Hastings chose me to sing in the theatrical. Even if it was in a silly mouse costume." She offered a feeble smile. "Still, it was hard not to think how things might have gone if Miss Hartfield had encouraged my singing when I was young. Then you came along." Again, she fixed her gaze on Dorinda. "Crowing about how proceeds from the theatrical were going to support the Children's Home. All the joy I'd felt, being onstage, just disappeared. Here I was, performing at last, and it was to benefit a place that nearly did me in."

"So you played some pranks," Jo said. "In hopes of disrupting the show and ruining Dorinda's fundraiser."

"Childish, I know." Tilly twisted her hands one over the other. "But you can't imagine how hard I've tried to forget how it was at the Children's Home. Then it all came flooding back. I felt like I was that little girl all over again. Bad Matilda who had no family, who was left out of everything."

"But you still wanted to sing in the theatrical, didn't you?" Dorinda asked.

"That's why you waited until after you sang the Midwinter song," Jo said. "To lure the cats inside. And to drop the sandbag."

"The bleak midwinter," Tilly said softly. "That was how it was for me at the Home. But you have to understand. I never meant for anyone to get hurt. The cats were a diversion, but the show went on. To stop it, I needed something bigger. While all you actors were busy on stage, I studied the ropes and pulleys that control the backdrops. When no one was looking, I climbed into the catwalks."

"Like you climbed trees when you were young," Dorinda said.

Tilly looked puzzled. "Yes. How did you know?"

"Lots of kids climb trees," Jo said quickly. Upset as Tilly was, there was no sense bringing up their talk with Cordelia Hartfield. Not when Tilly was trying to forget.

"I didn't mean to hurt anyone," Tilly said. "I started cutting the rope, and then I realized it was the wrong one, so I quit. I had no idea it was holding a sandbag. When it fell and knocked you over, I felt awful. I could hear Miss Harfield's voice in my head. She always used to say that if I kept playing pranks, someone was going to get hurt." She hung her head.

"It turned out all right," Jo said. "Just a sore shoulder and an ugly bruise."

Tilly looked up. "I'm so sorry. Truly I am. If I'd known what I know now, I'd never have tried out for that theatrical."

Jo squeezed her hand. “We’re glad you did.”

“Your singing adds so much to the show,” Dorinda said.

“My cookies.” Jumping up from her chair, Tilly hurried to take the sheet of cookies from the oven. Setting it aside to cool, she glanced at Jo and Dorinda. “I’ll be right back.”

When she was out of the kitchen, Jo leaned toward Dorinda. “You can’t bring Miss Hartfield tonight,” she whispered. “It would be too upsetting for Tilly.”

Subdued, Dorinda didn’t argue. “The whole situation is so sad. Miss Hartfield was only trying to help those children.”

“It’s clearer now, why she expressed those regrets. In retrospect, she must have realized how much damage she’d done, playing favorites. You need to get word to her. A message saying that you won’t be coming by tonight after all. Just don’t say anything about Tilly. Miss Hartfield doesn’t get out much. With any luck, Tilly will never find out she’s living here now.”

Dorinda nodded slowly. “I’ll take care of it.”

Tilly returned. Clasped close to her chest was the green book Noah had worked so hard to fashion. Handing it to Jo, she sat back down at the table. “At least it’s not too late for the final performance.”

“Noah will be so glad to see it. He couldn’t fathom what had become of it.”

“Maybe you could...find some reason for it to have gone missing besides my taking it? If people find out what I’ve done, they’ll want nothing to do with me. And I have few enough friends here as it is.”

“Your secret is safe with us,” Jo said. “Isn’t it Dorinda?”

“Yes. Yes, of course.”

Jo hoped Dorinda could follow through on that promise. When it came to gossip, she rivaled a telegraph line.

"I need to give this back too." Tilly opened her fisted hand on the table. In her palm was the missing sleighbell.

"I understand why you took the book," Jo said. "It was a vital part of the production that you wanted to stop. But why the sleighbell?"

Tears welled in Tilly's eyes. "As I said, Christmas wasn't a happy time for me at the Children's Home. But one Christmas Eve, when I was eight years old, we had a special visitor. She gathered all of us children around the fireplace, and I guess even Miss Hartfield was touched by the Christmas spirit that night, because she didn't try to exclude me, even though she'd caught me trying to sneak someone else's gift from under the tree earlier in the day. This stranger told us the most enchanting Christmas stories, and at each crucial moment, she'd ring a little sleighbell that hung from a red ribbon."

Plucking the sleighbell from her palm, Tilly jingled it, the joyful sound filling the kitchen.

"A happy memory for you," Dorinda said.

Tilly nodded. "The stranger must have noticed how her stories captivated me, especially the parts when she rang that bell. At the end of her visit, she gave that sleighbell to me. It was the best Christmas gift I ever received."

"Being singled out, but in a good way," Jo said.

"Yes." Tilly glanced away, then returned her gaze. "Sadly, the magic didn't last. On Christmas Day, when the other children opened their gifts, my old jealousies returned. I tore the arm off another girl's brand-new doll. As punishment, Miss Hartfield took the sleighbell away. Later, she tried to give it back, but I was too hardheaded to accept it."

"So you when you saw the bells on the theatrical's sleigh," Jo said, "you cut one off and clutched it in your hand while you sang."

Tilly cocked her head slightly, looking at her. "I didn't think anyone would notice. It gave me courage, I guess. To sing in front of all those people without them knowing the sort of person I really am." She gazed a moment at the bell, then pressed it into Jo's hand. "Take it, please. I won't be needing it anymore."

Chapter Ten

Approaching the alley behind Ross's Opera House, Jo tucked the green book under the flap of her coat, protecting it from the crystalline snowflakes that were beginning to fall from the woolly blanket of clouds overhead. In the warm glow of the gas lamps, she paused, tipping her head toward the sky, savoring the smattering of snow that dusted her cheeks.

A magical start to an evening of wonder. Or it would have been, if not for what was certain to be Tilly's absence. She dreaded breaking the news to Oliver Hastings.

Having crept out from behind the trash bins, the cats sat at her feet, tails swishing, seeming as mesmerized as she was by the flakes drifting from the sky. She bent to pet them. "I don't suppose either of you can sing?"

They stared at her blankly.

"I didn't think so." Straightening, she gripped the door handle. "Wish me luck."

Inside, she found the cast and crew in a festive mood. "Have you seen Noah?" she asked Will, who was adjusting the curled toes of his green felt slippers.

"Over there." Will nodded toward the far end of the stage. Wearing a red Santa's hat, Noah was crouched next to the sleigh, examining one of the runners.

Her red skirt swishing, Jo approached him. Concentrating as he was on the sleigh, she had to tap his shoulder to get his attention. "Quite the fetching hat you've got there," she said.

Tipping his head to look at her, he smiled. "Glad you like it. Oliver brought them for all the behind-the-scenes crew." He stood, facing her. "Just putting a bit of wax on the runners." He held up the bar of beeswax in his hand. "Can't have a squeaky sled."

"I should think not. I've brought you something." From inside her cloak, she withdrew the green book and handed it to him.

As if to affirm that it was real, he turned it over in his hands. "You found it."

"Not exactly. Tilly returned it. Along with this." Reaching in the pocket of her coat, she gave him the sleighbell.

"Tilly took these?"

"Yes. But you mustn't tell anyone. She's so embarrassed."

He shook his head. She had rarely seen him look so baffled. "Our Mouse in the Corner. What got into her?"

"Remember the night the book and the sleighbell went missing? Mr. Hastings had just told the cast about how the theatrical would benefit the Hartfield Children's Home. That's what set Tilly off. She grew up there, and while it might have been a wonderful experience for some of the children, just the mention of it brought back horrible memories for her."

"So she tried to shut down the production."

Jo nodded. "She didn't mean any harm. But from the sounds of it, she'd done her best to bury her memories from the orphanage, and then all of a sudden, with the Children's Home linked to the theatrical, the bad feelings came flooding back. She got in her head that by thwarting the production and ruining Dorinda's fundraiser, she might spare other children the experience she'd had."

"She just opened up and told you all this?"

"Not of her own accord. Dorinda heard a rumor about Tilly having grown up at the Children's Home, and things sort of snowballed from there. We ended up at Tilly's house, and she admitted to everything. The book and the sleighbell. Luring in the cats. Climbing into the catwalks to cut a rope that operated one of the backdrops. But she cut the wrong one."

"And by the time she realized her mistake, it was too late," Noah said. "The weight of the sandbag was enough to fray the rope where she'd started to cut it."

"She was horrified when the sandbag fell." Jo sighed. "The long and short of it is that you've got your props back, but now we're short one singer."

"Tilly's not coming tonight?"

Jo shook her head. "That sleighbell reminded her of the one happy memory she cherished from her time at the Home. She hung onto it while she sang. She said it gave her courage. I told her she could keep it, that it didn't matter that much to the show. But she insisted I take it. She said she doesn't need it anymore."

"But there's only this last performance," Noah said. "You couldn't talk her into coming?"

"I'm afraid not. I told her we wouldn't let word get out about what she'd done. You're the only one I'm going to tell, and I made Dorinda promise to keep the details to herself as well. Even so, I guess Tilly feels too ashamed to show up."

"Ashamed and unworthy, I'd guess. If only—"

"Ah, there you are, Jo." With his own red Santa hat askew on his head, Oliver Hastings hurried toward them. "I saw there were two costumes still in the wardrobe, and I feared some harm had come to our Winter Witch."

"I'm heading over now to get dressed." Jo drew a breath, steeling herself. "I'm guessing the other costume belongs to Tilly?"

"Why, yes," Hastings said. "How did you know?"

She and Noah exchanged glances. "I spoke with her earlier today. She indicated that she...she won't be able to make it tonight. She's terribly sorry."

Hastings pressed his hands to his cheeks. "No Mouse? No songs? Whatever shall we do?"

"We'll have to work around those parts. I'll let Amity know to come in on Tilly's Act Two cue, right after my line about the manor being all mine. And I'll see if she can start off the singing at the end. Amity's voice isn't quite as lovely as Tilly's, but unlike some of us, she can carry a tune."

"Yes, yes. I suppose that will have to do." Hastings clapped his hand on her shoulder, causing her to wince. "I appreciate your taking care of all that. I just don't see why Tilly didn't come to me herself."

"I think the...the circumstances that came up have been a bit overwhelming for her. So I took it upon myself to let you know."

With the matter settled, Hastings went off to find Lord Mistletoe. Jo tracked down Amity at the dressing table and filled her in on the revised plans for the evening. Amity had tried unsuccessfully to get Jo to explain earlier, when she was typing up the Children's Home article at the office, why she seemed so distracted. But wanting to keep her word as best she could to Tilly, Jo had deflected Amity's questions, and Amity had let the matter drop. Now, she asked for no details about Tilly's absence, remarking only that she hoped whatever had gone wrong would sort itself out.

Jo had the same hope. Maybe Tilly's handing out her gingerbread men to the millworkers' children would lift her spirits. Maybe later, after some time had passed, Jo could stop by her house without Dorinda, and they could chat like friends about anything except Tilly's past.

Hurriedly, she donned her white robe and did her make-up. When the show ended, she'd miss the theatrical's camaraderie and shared sense of purpose, but she would not miss the grease paint.

Remembering the cats' milk, she fetched the bowl and opened the can. Passing by the wardrobe closet on her way to the backdoor, she looked away, avoiding the mouse costume that hung forlornly there. Setting the bowl in the alley, she saw that the snow was coming more steadily now, the cats shaking it off their backs as they dived toward the milk.

Closing the back door firmly behind her, Jo was struck by the cheerful sounds of laughter and banter coming from the auditorium. It didn't sound as if the threat of snow had kept folks away. If anything, the chatter sounded louder than it had on previous nights. Astorians were used to inclement weather, and in December, any shift away from rain was bound to be met with some excitement.

Before long, the orchestra was winding down its truncated version of Beethoven's Ninth. The cast gathered in the wings, the actors from the first scene stage right, the others stage left. From behind a side curtain, Jo peered out at the audience. Most had taken their seats, but a few stragglers were still coming in.

She scanned the crowd, picking out familiar faces. Clara Shelton's grandmother, who kept a room for Clara at her house in town so she wouldn't have to take the ferry back and forth to Clatsop Spit when she had events here. Randolph Jenkins, who owned the competing newspaper. Stella Wisener, whose husband had left the *Register* to Jo, and Birdie Magness, who lived with Stella now. Stanley Osborne from the dry goods store. The town's seamstress, Mabel Parker. And tonight, Reverend Worthington had even brought his wife.

At last, Jo spied the faces she was looking for. Three rows up from the orchestra and two seats in from the aisle sat her father, Effie, and Pablo. She waggled her fingers at them even though she knew they couldn't see her. Then, to her surprise, she spotted Hattie and John Elliott coming down the aisle. On John's boots, she glimpsed a dusting of snow as he and Hattie slipped into the empty seats beside Jo's father. He looked pleased to see them but not surprised.

Did everyone but her know that Noah and Amity's parents had journeyed from Oysterville for tonight's performance? Evidently not. At the far end of the stage, Amity clapped her hands to her mouth, delight shining in her eyes.

So many people they knew and loved, all gathered to witness the Christmas magic. If only Jo had been able to stop Dorinda, that could have included Tilly.

The final notes of the symphony sounded, and the lights dimmed. As Reverend Worthington got up to give the invocation, Noah came up behind Jo, wrapping his arms around her waist.

She leaned into him. "Your parents are here," she whispered.

"So I saw," he said. "And that's not all. When I went to shut the wardrobe closet, the mouse costume was gone."

"Tilly's here? Where?" She twisted around, wanting to go to Tilly, to let her know how glad she was that she'd come after all.

"Not sure," Noah said. "Maybe in the dressing room."

She closed her eyes as Reverend Worthington began his invocation. *You did it, Tilly. You found your courage.*

When the prayer was finished, Dorinda took the stage. Clad in a full-skirted gown of green velvet, she launched into her announcement about how proceeds from tonight's performance would benefit the orphans at the Hartfield Children's Home. Emerging from backstage, Amity and Wesley took their places for the opening scene. The stagehands grabbed the ropes, ready to tug the curtains open.

Having heard Dorinda's appeal before, Jo was only half-listening. Then a deviation from the usual script caught her attention.

"Tonight, we have a special guest, right down here in the front row," Dorinda said. "Please join me in welcoming Cordelia Hartfield, founder of the Hartfield Children's Home."

Applause rose from the crowd. Illuminated by the orchestra's lights spilling over the front row of seats, Dorinda's beau, Warren Hatch, helped Miss Hartfield to her feet. Clad in a simple, cream-colored gown, she blinked into the lights, her lips turned in a prim smile.

Jo's heart sank. She'd been perfectly clear with Dorinda. Miss Hartfield was not to come tonight. If Tilly wasn't here, it wouldn't have mattered so much. But now that she had found the wherewithal to come, how could she possibly go onstage knowing that the woman who'd caused her so much pain was sitting right in the front row?

Aside from Noah, no one else knew enough to be as alarmed and upset as Jo was at that moment. But there was nothing to be done now. Once the show got underway, Jo checked the dressing room. It was empty. She checked with Clara, Will, and Felicity. None of them had seen Tilly.

There was nothing to do but go on. Onstage, the problem of the Winter Witch's hold on Mistletoe Manor was revealed. Tonight, when Eliza found the book in the library, it was not the old leather-bound fisheries book but Noah's lovely green volume, the gold foil runes gleaming in the stage lights.

With the appearance of Jingle and the forest sprites, the adventures began, though at every turn, Eliza and Jingle's efforts to defeat the spell came to naught.

Jo readied herself to take the stage. Without Tilly's song, her lines would lack some of their punch. She'd try to make up for that with her delivery.

But as she stepped forward toward the lights, a figure emerged from stage right. The Mouse in the Corner. Perhaps by some miracle, Tilly had missed Miss Hartfield's introduction.

Jo shrank back as Tilly lifted her face and began to sing. As always, the clarity of her voice was astounding, each note struck in perfect pitch. But tonight, as she sang with her hands unfisted, there was a special depth, a heartfelt sorrow so poignant it brought tears to Jo's eyes. The bleak winter. The moaning wind. The iron-hard earth, the stone-like water. Snow on snow on snow. Tilly's voice made all of it seem hauntingly real.

Long, long ago. Tilly held the last note for what seemed an eternity.

Applause resounded through the auditorium as the lights dimmed and the Mouse in the Corner receded into the darkness. Coming out her reverie, Jo hurried into place to deliver the Witch's lines.

Later, between onstage obligations, Jo looked again for Tilly but found no sign of her. Noah said he'd caught a glimpse of her leaving the stage, but he'd had to prepare for a scene change, and when he looked again, she was gone.

It wasn't until the final scene that Jo finally found her, or rather, she found Jo. As the cast gathered for the play's conclusion, Jo turned to see Tilly descending the spiral staircase that led to the catwalks.

Tilly came alongside her. Jo greeted her with a smile. "Your singing was magnificent tonight," she whispered.

"Thank you," Tilly said simply.

Jo debated whether she should say anything about Miss Hartfield. When they all went onstage for the final song, Tilly would only have to glance down at the orchestra, and she'd see her. The shock of it could well be too much.

"Tilly, there's someone here tonight you should know about."

"Cordelia Hartfield. I know. I heard Dorinda introduce her." Tilly paused. "I wasn't going to come tonight, you know. But when I was giving out those gingerbread men to the children, there was so much joy on their faces. And I thought, if my singing could bring that joy to even one person in the audience tonight, the rest of it wouldn't matter so much. I mean, the hurt wouldn't go away, but I didn't have to be that person anymore."

Jo squeezed her hand. "And you aren't."

"Coming from the dressing room, I heard Dorinda's announcement about Miss Hartfield," Tilly said. "I wasn't sure I could keep my resolve. But I went and sat in the dark and told myself I could step out into the light and trust my voice."

Jo nodded. Maybe Dorinda was right. Maybe Jo had been too quick to judge, to assume that once someone acted a certain way, they weren't capable of acting in another. With her courage tonight, Tilly had proven her wrong.

She wished she could explain her thoughts to Tilly, but the orchestra was cuing up for the final song. As scripted, Tilly led the cast on stage. But as they gathered in a semi-circle around her, the music abruptly stopped.

Onstage, every head turned as, from stage right, Cordelia Hartfield shuffled toward them, supported on one side by Warren and on the other by Dorinda. Passing by the rest of the cast, she stopped next to Tilly. She nodded curtly at Dorinda, who let go of her arm. Warren followed suit, and the two of them receded.

With a wobble in her step, Miss Hartfield reached her trembling fingers toward Tilly. Tentatively, Tilly took her hand.

Miss Hartfield cleared her throat. "My dear Matilda, of all the regrets I've had in my life, none have struck me deeper than knowing how poorly I treated you when you were in my care. I won't presume to ask your forgiveness. I was young and foolish and simpleminded about what I thought children needed. Somehow, in spite of all that, you've grown into a beautiful woman with a beautiful voice that has touched every heart here tonight."

Tears streamed down Tilly's face, her mouse whiskers running in streaks toward her chin. "I wasn't the easiest child."

"Easy or not, you deserved more love than you got." A tear streaked Miss Hartfield's pale cheek. She took an embroidered handkerchief from her pocket and dabbed at it. Then, reaching up, she wiped Tilly's face, drying her tears.

"All these years." Miss Hartfield returned the soiled handkerchief to her pocket. "All these years."

She seemed to have more to say, but when the words didn't come, she withdrew her fisted hand from her pocket. Unfurling her fingers, crooked with age, she held up a small sleighbell tied with a red ribbon.

Tilly gasped. "My bell."

"Your bell." Miss Hartfield jangled the bell, its silvered jingle melodic and sweet, then pressed it into Tilly's open hand.

Jo looked around at her friends. Not a dry eye to be seen. Even Oliver Hastings was dabbing his face with a handkerchief. Catching Dorinda's eye, she flashed a smile. For all Jo's trying to protect Tilly, Dorinda had done the right thing after all.

The orchestra started up the music again. As Tilly clung to Miss Hartfield's hand, her crystal-clear voice filled the auditorium. *Here we come a-Wassailing among the leaves so green.*

Clasping hands, the cast and crew chimed in. *Here we come a wandering, so fairly to be seen.*

A chorus of voices filled the auditorium as the audience joined in. *Love and joy come to you, and to you a Wassail too.*

Closing her eyes, Jo pictured the snow falling outside, the children spilling from their homes to build snowmen, the skating and the coasting, her picturesque little town transformed under a fleeting blanket of white. A Christmas to remember for all who called this place home.

AUTHOR'S NOTE

The magic of Christmas has captivated me since I was a child. Credit for that goes to my parents, who enriched our holiday with candles and music, and who widened our celebration to includes all sorts of seasonal festivities, including those associated with St. Nicholas Day, St. Lucia's Day, and Hanukkah.

Readers who are familiar with the Tidewater Chronicles know that I count myself fortunate to live near Astoria on the Oregon coast, within walking distance of the mighty Pacific Ocean. As the oldest English-speaking settlement west of the Rockies, Astoria has a long and rich history, with lots of material to draw from in these books. Nevertheless, this is a work of fiction, and any resemblance of the characters to real present-day people is coincidence.

One of my favorite sources for local period detail is Carol Carruthers Lambert's self-published family history *Letters from Louise.* From its pages, I've drawn period-appropriate Christmas presents for Jo to give her family and friends. Drawing from Louise's letters, Lambert offers rich details about the amateur theatricals the community put on. I also credit Louise and her letters with informing the snowfall in this book's concluding pages. These days, snow rarely falls in Astoria. But in the last decade of the nineteenth century, Louise writes of wintertime coasting on Astoria's snow-covered hills and skating on the lakes of Clatsop Plains, south of town.

My interest in orphans and orphanages comes in part from my own family's history. After her husband left her, my great-great-grandmother headed West, leaving four of their six children at a North Dakota orphanage. She ended up in Montana, where eventually she was reunited with most if not all of her children. The details are sketchy. In what she wrote of her remembrances from growing up, my great-grandmother makes no mention of her siblings having been left for orphans.

If you enjoyed this novella, you'll like the other Gilded Age mysteries in my Tidewater Chronicles series. Subscribers to my bimonthly newsletters are the first to learn about my latest books. In my newsletters, I also share deals and discounts. And when you sign up for the newsletter at www.vanessalind.com, you'll get a free novella to download.

Thanks for reading!

Vanessa Lind

Special Offer

Book endings are bittersweet, aren't they? You get attached to characters and their world. When the book ends, you're left wanting more. That's why I enjoy writing series.

Want to know more about how Ingrid met Sam and became part of the bookshop in the modern-day part of the Tidewater Chronicles? I've got a free novella telling that story, exclusive to newsletter subscribers. If that intrigues you, you can get it at https://dl.bookfunnel.com/lwklbsunp3

And if you find you're getting attached, don't worry. You can follow the characters you love through all the dual timeline mysteries in The Tidewater Chronicles.

Happy reading!

Vanessa Lind

www.vanessalind.com

More Books by Vanessa Lind

SECRETS OF THE BLUE AND GRAY

The Courier's Wife

Enemy Lines

Gray Waters

A Fond Hope

THE TIDEWATER CHRONICLES

The Shanghai Secret

The Shipwreck Secret

The Seance Secret

The Seamstress Secret

www.vanessalind.com

www.ingramcontent.com/pod-product-compliance
Ingram Content Group UK Ltd.
Pitfield, Milton Keynes, MK11 3LW, UK
UKHW042014190726
13854UKWH00005B/2277

9 798223 476481